CALIFORNIA LIFE

WILL SMITH

ISBN 978-1-3999-0075-1

Cover design by Eleanor Lloyd-Jones at Shower of Schmidt Designs.

To Liza.

For always pushing me to dream.

CONTENTS

1

ME, MYSELF & I

I would like to tell you about my life living on the west coast of America in beautiful, sunny California. This book has me as the main character and the other individuals I happen to meet along the way. I'm not one for following the standard rules of book writing. I just want to write my thoughts down and share them. That being said, how do I tell you all about me, myself, and of course I? Where do I start? We can all describe a person if someone asks us, "What's so and so like?". However, to describe one's self can be quite difficult. I'll try to be as open and as honest as I can. Anyways, here goes, please try to keep up.

Starting at the beginning, of course. William Smith is my full name, and I was born in Anfield, Liverpool, on the 8^{tth} of April 1972. The Anfield area of Liverpool is rundown like a lot of places up in the north of England. Liverpool mainly was a shipping port up to the end of the sixties. This explains why, except for London, Liverpool was the most severely bombed city during the Second World War. At the age of five, I was taken into care by the local authorities or social services. From the age of five, I was brought up in a variety of institutions, and for the next eleven years of my life, I spent moving from one placement to another. I lived primarily in a children's home on the Wirral called Wimbrick Hey, which was the type of place you go to for a short-term stay for up to six months.

I did spend some time at Bryn Allen School for unruly boys in North Wales. However, I didn't stay there for very long because the rumours I heard from the other lads about staff members frightened me. Instead, I went to a mini secure unit called Red Bank in Newton Le Willows. This is without mentioning all the various short-term stays, ranging from three to six months, in places dotted all around the UK.

I was called Scouse a lot, which is short for Scouser. It means a person who is born in Liverpool. Just to let you know, in England, if you were born in London, you got called a cockney; if you were born in Newcastle, you were called a Geordie. There are all sorts of reasons behind these regional names. The name Scousers comes from some Norwegian soup sailors had brought over back in the day. It is generally accepted that you either like Scousers or you don't, but what is always true is you'll never meet a more genuine type of person than a Scouser. We say it as we see it, and we don't hold back.

I have had a lot of ups and downs over the years. Like I'm sure most kids did, once I became old enough to realise what was going on, I became rebellious. In an attempt to beat the system and fight back in any way possible, I started running away from these children's homes. Before long, I had been classified as a persistent absconder. The court system, well, the juvenile court system, decided that it was in my best interests to rehouse me in a secure unit in Newton Le Willows called Redbank.

So, from the age of eleven, I was locked in, almost like a prison. In the secure unit I was held in, there were eight people in total. Over time, I learnt I was the only one there who hadn't committed a crime. I was locked up to protect myself according to the courts, the police, and social services. Now that I am older, I understand why I was placed in a secure unit, but at the time, I thought the world hated me. Any respect I had for social services, the court system, or the police was gone. I thought, how could they lock an eleven-year-old boy in a cell?

By the age of eleven, I was five foot ten and weighed over one hundred and twelve pounds or eight stone. I was big for my age. I made things as difficult as possible for the next five years of my life by constantly keeping the staff at Redbank on their toes. If I was given an opportunity to cause mayhem or trouble, I did so gladly. I knew I would get slapped about or put in a strip cell for twenty-four hours, but I didn't care. I carried on regardless. I wasn't fazed or bothered in the slightest by these punishments.

When I turned fifteen in the later part of eighty-eight, I met with Mr Martindale, the governor of Redbank, and my social worker, Maureen. I was sat at a table in a brightly lit room, and my files were presented to me. These pieces of paper that Redbank had kept on me for the past five years detailed all infractions and mundane happenings of my life there. Anything from me attempting to escape to the paracetamol pills I was given by the doctor for a headache a few years ago. I had tried to abscond that many times that they made me wear a jacket and trousers with a bright yellow strip down them constantly. This was so I would be noticed easily if I did manage to get out.

The second file, which was more like a huge book that Maureen was holding, contained all my notes that social services had taken over the last eleven years. These included every court case I'd been involved in since the age of five onwards. They gave details of all the outcomes, my age at the time, and where I was located. Everything about my life was in here, and there were even sections about my parents. As I started to look at the files, Mr Martindale said, "Will, both I and Maureen need to talk to you about when you turn sixteen and what your next step will be in life?" I sat and listened to what they both had to say, but all the while, I was dying to read my file. The courts had listened to social service's recommendations and had granted their request that I would be allowed to leave Redbank and head back over to the Wirral and Wimbrick Hey, the place I had first stayed in all those years ago. Upon my sixteenth birthday, I would be released into a bed-and-breakfast that social services would sort out for me. I would be given a fifty-pound clothing voucher to buy clothes for when I leave. I heard what both of them had to say. It wasn't like I had a choice because this had already been decided for me. I reached forward and pulled the two files closer.

I was done with this conversation. As I began to start reading the file from Maureen, I saw Mr Martindale getting up from his seat and the social worker following, "William, you take all the time you need to read them. You can stay in here the rest of the day if you wish," he said, as he walked towards the door. I didn't respond but looked up to let him know I'd heard what he said. He smiled at me and opened the door.

Once they both left the room, I opened up the social services file. The first thing I noticed was that my file hadn't been started in 1977 when I was five years old but had begun two years prior, in 1975. I was only around three, then I supposed. I read how social services had been called out to an address I had never heard of in Liverpool. The parents, who turned out to be my own, were both intoxicated to the extent that the infant (me) was taken for the night until they had both sobered up and were able to collect me. According to the file over the course of 75 and the following year of 76, this same incident reoccurred eight times.

One set of notes said that Merseyside police were called to a house for an unattended child. Both the Police and social services spoke at my child hearing, to which I was obviously too young to even recall after all these years.

In 1977, there was an order placed by the court removing any rights my parents had over me. I was handed over into the care of the local authority. From 1977 until the latter part of 1980, there were many court cases and paperwork, but it looks like by December, the court had decided I would no longer be going back to my parents. I was now eligible to be placed up for adoption. After this, I would spend the rest of my childhood in care.

I continued searching through my file. Within it, there was

another file with my name on it: William Smith. However, this wasn't me; it was my father. I read through it all and tried to absorb as much as I could. Up till now, I had heard nothing about my parents or if I had any siblings. Every time I asked, the answer was avoided. I continued reading about how he and my mother, Eileen Smith, had been arrested on numerous occasions for being drunk in public or being a nuisance. They had even been arrested for affray after hitting people who were leaving a bingo hall. They both had tried to fight the court's decisions, but in 1988 they had exhausted their last battle. I had no idea what their last known address was in Liverpool, but I memorised it to write it down when I got back to my cell. 25 Stockbridge Street, Anfield.

I carried on searching and found a visitor's list. This contained all the people that had visited me since 1977 up to this very day. In seventy-seven, my parents came twice; then once in April, on my birthday, of course, and then again in July. They are the only two dates that they visited I could find. I looked down the list. It was mostly a lot of social worker visits and counsellor meetings until I came to some names I didn't know in 81 and once more in 83. In 81, the name was Mr and Mrs Stanley. In the notes, to the side of their name was a description of the meeting. They had come to see about adopting me, along with the Hutches, in 83. But, I'm still here, I thought, so they didn't want me. I laughed. *Who would? I'm nothing but trouble.* I spent the rest of the afternoon reading my file over and over as if I was trying to memorise it all. I read what previous staff in Redbank and Social Services had written about me:-

"William has learnt how to bend and flex the system to work in his favour." Mr Track Redbank (retired)

"Will is capable of manipulating any situation he's put in, so it works best for him. He can no longer be trusted; he has become out of control and a liability to himself and others around him. Cheryl Hughes, social worker 81-83. This explains my move to Redbank, and I laughed. I don't even remember a social worker called Mrs or Ms Hughes.

One teacher even wrote, "William's intelligence level is astounding for someone so young." I couldn't make out whose scribbled signature it was, more than likely a teacher from Critchley house in Dorset.

Brendan Walsh wrote, "William is an extraordinary thinker; he has an ability to adapt to any situation."Headmaster Bryn Allen. "William has been trouble since he came here, fighting since his first day and constantly causing trouble with other pupils." Mr Lally, headteacher, St Marys School.

I heard how some comments were saying, I was alright and just needed help, to others saying I was too late for help. I've picked out the best ones, well, the ones I thought sounded true and unbiased.

About 4.30 that afternoon, both Mr Martindale and Maureen came back into the room. Maureen asked me how "I was."

"I'm fine. Can I ask you something?" I blurted out. Before she had a chance even to hear what I had asked for, "In my file, it says I had no visits from my parents after seventy-seven, how come?"

She responded with, "they just never came again, Will, sorry."

"Hey, it's alright. I'm not sorry." I laughed. They weren't parents, I thought to myself. I walked out of the room and back to my cell. I wrote their last known address down, anyway. A few days later, I was packing up and heading to Wimbrick Hey. I hadn't seen much sunlight in the last four years, only from the window in my cell and the hour of exercise I was allowed each day. Don't get me wrong, Redbank isn't a prison, but it's damn close. You're allowed out to work. I was a cleaner that mopped the halls in the day. The same halls day in, day out. In the evening, we go to a TV room until eight pm, then back to our cells. Lights would go out at nine pm, and the next day is the same. "Routine," as the staff would always say.

My last month in Wimbrick Hey flew by, and before I knew it, I was sixteen and being released. I was ready to take the world on. I could now start to live my life without having to answer to anyone. Sleep till I want, go to bed when I want, basically do what I wanted when I wanted.

On my sixteenth birthday, Maureen showed up and drove me to a bed-and-breakfast in Secombe. As we pulled up in her car, she said, "the room was above a cafe, the cosy corner cafe to be exact, must be as it's on the corner." She chuckled out loud in nervous anticipation that I would laugh as well.

You have to go round back and enter from the alleyway to get in. Maureen had the keys already from the landlord and showed me to my room. It was a dump. The couch in my room was all ripped, and the bed looked like it had been there since the building was put up. There was a nightstand and a wardrobe that had been brand new in 1950. The wardrobe was leaning on the wall for support to hold itself up by the looks of it. The room itself appeared to be dark, even though the curtains were open. It was very musty as if no one had been in the room for quite a while. Maureen showed me around the place. There was a kitchen on the middle floor that also appeared dark and dim until Maureen flicked the light on. It wasn't clean like I'm used to, but I didn't care. There was a small TV room located in the front of the property. At least, this was a bright room, being at the front of the building, it caught the most sun. The room only had a couch and a TV in it.

She told me breakfast is before ten each morning, except for Sunday. "You're on your own that day. You'll have to take yourself next door to the café," she said. After a few more minutes, she got to the front door and told me if I needed anything to call her at the office. After a quick hug, she walked away, and I never saw Maureen again. I had spoken to her on the telephone a few times, but as soon as I realised she could no longer do anything for me, I stopped calling. I was now completely alone.

I would like it to be known, this isn't a "Woe is me" story. I'm not attempting to pull on your heartstrings or even make you feel for me. You see, to me, this was just my life. I didn't know any different. I don't feel as if I've had a rougher upbringing than others. I just think I've had a different upbringing, is all.

So here, I'm stood at sixteen, with the clothes on my back. I have no education. Well, nothing I could place in the hand of a future employer anyway. Don't get me wrong, I'm far from stupid. I just got a different type of educational knowledge growing up. I learnt things that aren't in any schoolbooks. What I lacked in book smarts, I made up for in confidence and had what they called 'the gift of the gab'. I say confidence, but not cocky, just sure of myself. If I say I'm going to do something, I'm doing it. We can all become a little cocky from times, but I learnt to reign that in at a very early age. I always could think fast on my feet in any situation that arises. Not only do I think fast, but I have the capabilities to adjust to my surroundings easily. I sometimes feel like a leopard that's constantly changing its spots. It's just the way I learnt to survive growing up. It's not something you see at the time as being a bad thing, it's just the way life is right now.

Maureen had at least sorted out the unemployment stuff, so my rent was fully paid till I turned eighteen. I was given a family allowance book that I'm to take to the post office each week, and they give me sixty-nine pounds. Needless to say, "I was a king for a day on postie day." I spent the rest of the week completely broke until I somewhat figured out how to use money a little better. No one had taught me the cost of things or the value of items. This was all new and took some adjusting.

For the next two years or so, I spent it living life the way I wanted to live. I fell a lot but always got back up. I experimented with all the "do's" and 'don'ts' and even enjoyed some of these. I learnt a few lessons in life, such as never to trust anyone, as everyone is out for themselves. I dealt with unforgiving people. I got punished a few times for pushing boundaries but isn't that just life. I soon became quite adept at playing with fire, but without getting burnt. I also learnt that life hasn't a clue, that now isn't the time to hit you with a surprise, it just hits you, and you must learn to deal with it at the time. I dated a few girlfriends along the way, but to be fair, it wasn't like I put any effort into them once I'd achieved my goal.

After settling in above the corner cafe, I made a journey over the water to Liverpool. I decided to visit the last known address of my parents, 25 Stockbridge Street Anfield, which I had memorised from my files. The house was empty when I got there, but an elderly lady across the street shouted over to me. "If you're looking for Bill and Eileen, they're in the Shankly, the pub round the corner."

I thanked her as I walked in the direction she pointed. I entered the pub and ordered myself a pint, and stood at the bar. The place only had five people in it, including me and the bartender, a seriously worn older lady in a pair of faded jeans, a t-shirt, and flip-flops. A young lad who was engrossed in the slot machine by the door and a couple in their forties sat at a table. I sat there for most of the afternoon and even joined in the conversation that Eileen and Bill held with the bartender. I could see how these two lived in the pub. My dad, Bill, was old before his time, and the clothes he wore were rags. He hadn't shaved in days. To be honest, he might not have washed either, for all I knew. My mother, Eileen, was sitting in a pair of ripped jeans and a t-shirt. Her hair was greasy as if she hadn't washed it in weeks. I spoke to them throughout the afternoon. I never told them who I was. I gave them the false name, John when Bill had asked and tried to buy me a pint. I said no thanks, as I was leaving now. When I left and headed towards the bus stop to head back over the water to the cosy corner café, I knew that was it. I had met them, and that was all I wanted to do. Now that's the end of that.

Life carried on as it had done for a while, but before my nineteenth birthday, my circle of friends had changed so much. I wasn't able to keep friends for long. I'd usually mistreat them or something along those lines. Being brought up in care had made me reserved on the inside. On the outside, I looked and appeared as strong as an ox. Socially, I wasn't good at keeping friends as most were just associates with the Redbank experience alone. To be honest, being locked in a cell every night was enough to make anyone a little antisocial.

One morning, I sat in the cafe below my room and heard two guys a little older than me talking to each other about Holland. I listened, as I had heard of this place before. It wasn't long till I had joined the conversation, and for a brew, these two lads told me their stories. They got a passport from the post office for twelve pounds, then hitchhiked down to Dover and bought tickets to Rotterdam in Holland. They went on to tell me how they had smoked the best weed in the world and become so green after smoking it. They laughed together as one of them said, "best holiday we've ever had." I was amazed they did all that so easily. I'm doing this; I thought as I listened to every detail they told me. I put my plan into effect immediately. I decided I would be in France before the hour was up.

It took me a couple of weeks before I had arrived in Calais. As I walked away from passport control, I thought to myself. I was no longer that young lad entering Redbank and smiled.

I was now 18 and grown a little at 6ft 1 tall and two hundred and twenty-five pounds in weight. I spent the next three years travelling around Europe. I worked a variety of jobs to get by. I picked grapes in the south of France, stayed in a fly-infested caravan in a cow field that was freezing at night. It had perks though, for instance, I could drink all the wine I wanted. Unfortunately, this finished because it was only seasonal work, but I was relieved after having up to two bottles of wine a night to tell you the truth.

I worked in a cheese factory in Gouda, Holland. I had got this job from a couple of Scottish girls I had met in a rundown squat the British had taken over and claimed as their own. They both worked there and put a word in for me. I lived off Gouda cheese for months. I don't think I left there once without a block or two of cheese hidden upon my person.

I had a painting job in Germany. This paid very well and came with accommodation. I learnt a lot in this job, the German workers I'd been put with came just to work, and they knew just how to do a day's graft. At first, I was pretty much the tea maker, but I was left to do houses by myself before long. I lost the lot in the end for hitting my employer over a stupid football game and after a day on the beer. I also learnt that some people don't forgive and forget.

I worked in a fish factory in Italy, boning fish. This job, I hated. I couldn't get rid of the smell, and before I knew it, I'd quit. There was no chance at all of any sexual activities with me smelling like "Eau De Fish Guts."

When I couldn't find work, I would beg on the streets. I'm not proud of it. I would do whatever it took to survive. I stole whenever opportunities arrived. Life could be challenging at times, but I didn't mind. Although it had its good and bad points, I was living a life most only dreamed about. By February of 1997, I had had enough of sleeping rough and bumming my way around. Work became harder and harder to find, so I decided to head back home. Well, my place of origins anyway.

I arrived back in Secombe after nearly five years had passed. Nothing about Secombe had changed. I attempted to get my old room back in the cosy café, but it was rented, and the place was full. I laughed at this and remembered I was on the streets in Europe. It took me a few days of sleeping here and there when I saw a sign for a one bed flat. I rang the doorbell and spoke with the landlord. I explained I'd just come back from Europe and apologised for my appearance. "I've been travelling for two days," I told him. I did play it up and tell him I was sleeping in a park up the road. The room was mine before I had even finished my pleading case. I moved in that night.

I hooked up with some old friends I'd met before I went to Europe, but most had already been lost to 'the needle of dreams', as they say. Heroin was everywhere in those days. I was told of friends I'd known going too far and had overdosed and passed away. I heard how two others were locked up in prison for stealing to feed the habit. This was one of the "do's and 'don'ts" I had told you about. I avoided this and anyone that offered me any.

I quickly fell back into a routine in the UK and was back on unemployment again. Housing benefits coved my rent on the flat. I managed to get most of the furniture delivered free from the Salvation Army and even got bedding for pennies as the old women felt sorry for me. I decided to start a gardening business to bring in a little more money. It would have to be hush-hush as I didn't want the unemployment getting stopped. I could no longer just live on forty-four pounds and fifty pence a week. When I had the family allowance money, I had more money than this. I know I was a minor, but how can a grown man feed himself and purchase clothing, all on the government's pittance? Don't get me wrong, I was happy to take the money. I'd tried repeatedly to find employment, but it was impossible to find any type of work on the Wirral. I knew people who had an education and paperwork to prove it. Even with GCSEs and O levels, they couldn't find a job. I needed a little extra cash each week just to stay afloat. The gardening work took off. It's amazing how many people don't want to do gardening themselves on their weekends off. It was easier to pay me ten pounds a fortnight than listen to their wives moaning, which in turn allowed them to have relaxing weekends. I worked in all weather conditions.

In April, I only recall it being April because it was my birthday two days earlier. I watched a television show all about the state of California in America, home to the stars. The weather looked amazing, and palm trees lined the street. My mind started to think. I survived in Europe, barely. I laughed out loud to myself. As if this had amused me, could I do it again? But this time in America? Why not? I sat eating chips on the couch. I decided right there, and then I was going to California. I went to the post office the following morning after doing the dishes in the cafe for my breakfast. I ordered myself a passport and set about saving.

I kept my life quiet from this point on. I watched TV in the evenings and worked as much as I could during the day. I knew every penny I made was going towards America. I had raised the five hundred flight fare by the end of May, so I booked my ticket. The travel date was set for Thursday, the 27th of November, at one o'clock in the morning. My new passport had arrived at the beginning of September, and to emphasise the importance, it was the first time I had ever had a recorded delivery. I even had to sign a special card the postman presented to me. I ripped the envelope open so fast my new passport fell out onto the floor. I picked it up and opened it. This wasn't a cheap paper post office one, this was a leather-bound booklet. I became all excited just by seeing this. From that day on, I worked as many hours as I could. I didn't care if it was raining. I still went out and worked. Nearer to the end of November, around 1997, I sold all my possessions. I couldn't take it with me and gave away the rest to anyone who would take it.

This was the type of person Will Smith had grown up to become; who I am. Me, Myself, and I.

On the last day of August in 1997, Princess Diane died in a tragic car crash involving the media, or paparazzi, which was how the BBC had described them on the news. This shocked the people of the United Kingdom. This happened just three months short of my flight to America. On Sunday, I headed to the pub to have a drink for Diane. The pubs were packed, so I only had one. Some days will stay etched on your mind forever. Also, that year JK Rowling started releasing the Harry Potter books, and Titanic had come out at the movies. The current president was Bill Clinton, and he was starting his second term in the White House. I only tell you this so you can backtrack to the year in your minds.

Let's continue back to the story of what happened next, the experience that changed my life forever.....

2

LOS ANGELES

I walked through the double glass doors, which separated in the middle automatically as I approached. Coming from an air-conditioned airport terminal, I could instantly feel the heat difference, which was initially a shock to my lungs as the intake of warm air filled them. The sun was setting, and dusk was near. There was an orange glow in the sky. I adjusted the backpack I had thrown over my right shoulder in my excitement to get out of the airport and stepped out onto the sidewalk. This was my first look at America. Well, sunny California anyway. You could sense the importance in people as they scurried about, pulling, or carrying their cases. The road at the end of the sidewalk was three lanes across and a one-way system. It was end to end in cars, pickup trucks, and buses.

I reached with my left hand into the rear pocket of my jeans and pulled out my cigarettes. I had put them in my pocket as I stood up from my seat to exit the plane. As I steadied the backpack strap with my right hand to balance its weight, I flipped open the lid and pulled one out. Only then did I recall my lighter dying in the smoking lounge in Paris as I waited for my connecting flight from the United Kingdom. After travelling for so long, my nerves were shot, and I needed the sweet release of nicotine to relax me.

I looked around at the people standing on the sidewalk for someone I could catch a light. Directly in front of me, I could see a woman in her late 30s carrying a small infant that could not have been more than six months old. As cute as the baby was, I'm figuring in my head that a new mummy isn't likely to be a smoker. To my left was a gentleman standing with his back towards me along the side of the terminal building, leaning forward onto his luggage cart. I could see he was smoking by the cloud that was lingering in the air above him. I began my walk towards him, and my eye caught sight of his luggage. All his cases were matching and looked like they might have been real leather. Judging by the style and quality, they couldn't have been anything I could afford. Instead, all I had was my shoulder backpack I had found on a bench at a train platform in Salzburg, Germany, a few years back in ninety-three. I remember chuckling to myself back then as I had claimed it as mine instead of handing it in like most people would have done.

Once I got closer to this gentleman, I caught the smell of the cigarette he was smoking; it reawakened my senses after the thirteen-hour flight. My nose was drawn to this aroma because it knew my lungs needed this. Rather quite loudly, I found myself saying, "EXCUSE ME, YOU GOT A LIGHT MATE." I realised I had half-shouted this request, even startling myself a little with the deepness of my voice. It had, however, been a long day and a long flight. The gentleman turned his head away to look in the window he was standing next to, using it as a mirror. I caught his reflection in the windowpane, but not clearly enough to make out his features.

In what seemed like one move, the man turned his head towards me and stood directly up to meet me as I grew closer as if he was also startled by my previous tone.

I said to him as I came to a stop, "Sorry mate, I didn't mean to shout at you. I think I'm tired." I paused for a split second. "I didn't get much sleep on that plane, too many screaming kids. You got a light?" I enquired as I raised a cigarette to my hand and up to my lips.

"Yeah, sure, Bud," he replied with what was a very relaxing voice as if he had all the time in the world. He reached his right hand into his trouser pocket. I quickly looked at this man as he pulled out a Zippo lighter from his pocket and handed it to me. He appeared to be about my age, twenty-five, give or take a few years. Possibly a little older, but not much more than that. His head was shaven on the sides and spiked on top, not a crew cut per se, but more a military-style haircut; short, manageable, and smart in appearance. He had either not long ago wet his hair or used a wet look gel from the shine of it. His face was clean-shaven and suntanned. He was shorter than me, roughly about 5ft 8. I found a lot of people were generally shorter than me, being 6ft 1. He weighed approximately 220 lbs, about the same as me; however, he did appear to carry a little extra weight, not fat, but a bit flabby around the edges. He wore a light yellow, short-sleeved button-down shirt that looked freshly pressed, indicating he did not fly in it but had changed it recently. The same was true of his trousers. They appeared to have been newly pressed. These were light brown in colour, pleated and very smart, but still casual looking. His shoes were a darker brown than his trousers: soft leather that looked very comfy. I stood next to him in my jeans and a black Guinness t-shirt, I got free as a giveaway in my local boozer one night, and my new Adidas trainers I'd bought especially for this trip. To me, I looked smart and casual. This was my style of dress, who I was really. This would be classed as my Sunday best, what I'm wearing if I go out. The man asked me as I began to light my smoke, "Are you from England?"

I took a long, much-needed inhale as I replied, "yeah, Liverpool, you from California?"

"The Beatles," he responded as if he knew Liverpool. I had heard this a million times on my travels around Europe. I sent a half-smile his way. "No," he said. "I'm from San Antonio."

I looked at him strangely, as I had no idea where San Antonio was. This must have been obvious on my face as he quickly said, "I'm from the lone state, Texas," and smiled towards me.

"Oh," I responded while I looked out at the busy street, "so what ya doing out in California, business?". My body was shaking from the adrenaline of being free and having made it out here. It could also have been from the sudden rush of nicotine; I couldn't tell.

"No, no. I live here now, long story......you here on vacation?" he asked me.

I chuckled loudly. "Yeah, something like that."

He looked at me all strange, then smiled as if he hadn't fully understood me.

"So, which part of Cali are you staying in?" he said.

I told him my plans, well, the plans I had made before my trip to America, which was to stay on a beach or find a bus station to crash in until I could figure out my next step.

He looked at me like I was crazy, like I had no idea. "So you came here with nowhere booked to stay at?" he asked.

"I've had enough of England' I told him. 'I've travelled around Europe, so now I'm coming this way to have a look. I figured I would stay on the beach or at a train station until I managed to get situated and find work. I'm a hard worker, and someone will give me a job.'

"Damn," he said, with a slightly raised voice. "You have a set of balls on you."

I laughed, and he joined me, laughing towards the end. He asked, "So where are you staying tonight?" and he quickly looked at his watch, which I hadn't noticed earlier as it had been on his left wrist and was hidden by his body and the luggage cart.

I replied confidently. "I've heard that Long beach has beaches that are that hot it's impossible to walk on the sand without shoes." I'd read this in a magazine a few years back, but it had stuck in my head. "I'll probably stay around here at the airport tonight, and tomorrow once I get up, I'll figure a way to get to Long beach." *I'm sure someone at this airport will be driving towards Long beach,* I thought. I'd thumb a lift. This had worked for me in England and Europe, so why not.

He looked at me as if he was in shock, but with a small thought in the back of his head that I might be joking with him. So he looked towards me again and then replied with, "You're serious, aren't you?". He could now read my face clearly and knew I was.

"Yeah, of course, I am." I smiled at him.

This has been my plan to move to California since the idea sprung into my head last April while I sat on the sofa in my one-bedroom flat eating a bag of chips I'd grabbed on my way home from the pub.

He looked at me in awe. He said, "Wow, Buddy, so you have just flown over to another country to start a new life." I'm unsure if he thought of me as foolish, but he said, "Long Beach isn't really a nice place bud, the place is full of gangs." He looked right at me now and said. "You watch yourself downtown there."

He followed with, "I'm Joe, by the way." Joe placed his hand towards me, waiting for my hand to reciprocate to meet him. As it did, I caught myself hesitating, as if my name was the wrong thing to say. As my hand reached him, I felt the firmness of his grip as we shook hands.

I responded, "Alright, I'm William, well I get called Will," and smiled. "Nice to meet you, Joe," I said as our hands separated and my arm drew back towards my side.

He reached into his pocket and pulled out his cigarettes and lighter, offering the pack towards me with a smile, "Do you want one, William?"

I leaned forward and, in doing so, said, "yes, please, Joe, please call me Will, though. I get called William when I'm being told off." I pulled one from the packet and passed the pack back toward him with a smirk on my face. "Marlboro. I don't think I've ever smoked one of these," I said to him.

"They're ok really, Will," he informed me as he flipped open the Zippo lighter again and leaned in to light my smoke.

Just then, we heard a ringing. Joe said, "Excuse me, Will," and reached inside his pocket to take out his phone.

"Hello, hello."

I heard him saying before the sound of the traffic passing became too loud.

I was here; I had made it. I felt excited, like a child, in a way. All those extra gardening jobs I'd done in the rain and cold had finally paid out. I had £150 in English money, just short of $200 American dollars in my wallet. I had no bank cards; well, I wasn't counting the Lloyd's bank checking card, I had to make myself look good. It had expired last April anyways, but I hadn't yet thrown it out of my wallet. I'm going to have to find somewhere quiet to sleep tonight, but at least it's warm, was my next flashing thought.

Just then, Joe walked back towards me. "Sorry about that, Will' acknowledging the phone call as rude 'that was Lou, he's my airport pick up," "He's already here. He said he's outside terminal five, so he'll be here in a few seconds,' and turned his head towards the upcoming traffic.

"Nice." I paused for a second. "Well, good to meet you mate, catch ya around." I reached down to retrieve my backpack from the side of the window.

Then Joe said, "Hey Will if you don't have anywhere at all to stay tonight, you can sleep at mine. It takes some guts to do what you're doing. I'm not too far from here. Just up in Calabasas." My first thought coming from the mind of a 25-year-old man was… is he gay? Does he fancy me or something? He hadn't given me this impression of himself when we spoke. It must be in my mind. "Are you sure, Joe?" I responded excitingly.

"Come on, Will, grab your bag," he shouted over the noise of the black town car pulling up.

I grabbed my backpack, slung it over my shoulder, and rushed towards the car. The driver, took my backpack and put it in the boot. He walked to the rear passage door and opened it. "Mr Dicorpo," he gestured with his left hand as if he was inviting Joe into the car. Joe walked up to the side and slid into the seat. I followed him and was now sitting in the car alongside him. The driver closed the door firmly, turned, pulled the side door open, and climbed into his seat. The car started, and before I knew it, we were pulling away from the curb side and joining traffic. Joe looked at me and could see I was taking everything in and smiled. He leaned toward a phone on the side of the car wall and lifted it from the receiver.

"Lou," he said, "could you open the sunroof please, this is Will's first time in California." I looked towards the front of the car.I could just make out Lou's head and then realised a piece of glass separating the driver and his guests.

"Hey, Will, you can stand up if you want," said Joe.

I jumped straight to my feet and popped the top half of my body out the roof. The air was warm as it passed over my face. The terminal buildings are all lit up and seem very bright in the dusky evening. We left the airport, and I felt a light tap on my leg. I lowered my head, and Joe said, "this is Sepulveda boulevard it's huge. Once we join onto the freeway, you have to sit down, Will," he said. "But enjoy it while you can." I took in my surroundings with anticipation, as everything looked different. Even the buildings and storefronts were not like what I was used to back home. The weather, though, was amazing. I felt happy and loved the heat on my face as the car turned onto a road with a huge blue sign: 405 freeway. I knew it was time to sit back down now. Once I sat down in my seat, I could see Joe reaching for the phone again. As he picked it up and said, "Lou, can you close the roof please?" Lou gave Joe a thumbs up in acknowledgement. "Do you want a drink, Will?" Joe asked as he reached inside the cooler below the phone and placed his hand on a bottle of Budweiser.

"Yes, please, Joe," I said as I reached my hand to grab the bottle. "It won't take long to get there; traffic is flying now, rush hour is over." I smiled at Joe and turned to look out the window as we flew along the freeway. I noticed how different the cars looked. We passed cars I'd never heard of and laughed as I thought there was no chance of seeing a Robin Reliant or Morris Minor here. Joe didn't say much more during the drive. I think he was also tired from his flight, but also he knew to leave me to take it all in. As we exited the freeway, there was no more street lighting. We were climbing a hill, and it was pitch black outside. It appeared as if we were going up a mountain. Once we got closer to the top, Joe reached into his shirt pocket and pulled out a plastic gate clicker. As he clicked it, the large gate in front of the upcoming car began to open.

"This is Canyon Drive, Will. My place." I didn't respond. I just stared at Joe to let him know I'd heard him talking. The car pulled past the gate and continued up a small hill until we reached the top and the road became flat again. I could now see the house was huge. A lot bigger than I was expecting, but being fair, I had no idea what to expect, and in my mind, I would have been happy with a two up and two down. As the car came to a halt outside the front door, Lou jumped out and rushed back to open my door. I thanked him as he opened Joe's door.

"There you go Mr. Dicorpo, home, and you can rest now."

Joe chuckled. "have a good drink, more like," as he passed the Budweiser bottle that was still in his hand to Lou.

Lou sped around and unloaded the cases, and placed them at the front door. My backpack stood to the side of Joe's luggage. I followed Joe to the door. "Thanks, Lou," Joe said as he passed him some money. I've no idea how much.

Lou replied, "thank you so much, Mr. Dicorpo. I'll see you soon. Have a lovely evening." He smiled at me and made his way back to the car, and entered the driver's seat. As Lou pulled away from the front door, Joe said to me, "come on, Will, let's get in and have a drink."

As we entered the hall, Joe clicked on the lights, and the whole place lit right up. It was mostly open plan, and you could see from the hall that to the right was the living room, which had a wide corridor at the rear of the room. This must be the way to the bedroom, and the left was the kitchen. The middle section between the kitchen and the living room was a continuation of the hallway, with two large glass patio doors covering nearly the whole wall. These must lead out to the garden, I thought. "Drop your bag there, and let's grab a beer."

As he walked towards the kitchen area, I followed him; a beer sounded perfect right about now. As we entered the kitchen, Joe headed towards the fridge, which, I have to say, was massive. I looked around as Joe passed the island in the centre and headed towards the fridge. I felt as if I was stood in a huge hotel kitchen, not that I had stood in many of them before. I looked towards the oven, which looked like it was made of solid iron, and you just knew that it wasn't easy to move in. It was clear this was the main room in the house. The kitchen looked lived in.

Joe headed towards me and passed me a bottle of Coors Light. I hadn't even heard of Coors, never mind light. As I raised it to my lips, Joe passed me and, as he was walking out the room, said, "let me show you around quickly." He pointed towards the corridor off the kitchen and said to me, "Down there is a toilet, laundry room, and garage." He turned and went straight towards the front room, which was opposite. As we walked through the living room and towards the corridor, I looked at the huge L shaped leather couch. The TV was bigger than I had seen before. As Joe came to the first door on the right, he opened it and told me it was the restroom. I knew this meant toilet already. We continued to the next door on the left, and Joe said, "this is your room, Will, it's got an ensuite in it, so you can shower no problem." He turned the light on, and I looked in. I've lived in smaller houses than this room, I thought. Joe pointed down the corridor to another door on my left and said, "that's Cameron's room. She stays whenever she wants to. The last room is the master suite that's my room." He walked past me as I reached in to look at the room I was staying in.

The bed was made, and at the foot was another pair of glass patio doors. I switched the light off and headed out into the corridor behind Joe. He walked to the large glass doors in the hallway, switched on the outside lights, unlocked the door, and slid it open. I immediately felt the heat difference as Joe, and I stepped out onto the patio. I could hear water running, and looking over to my right, I saw there was a swimming pool and a hot tub at the side of it, complete with a patio and table and chairs. The patio looked as if it continued past my bedroom doors as if the house was designed with the pool in mind; go for a swim, then go back to your room.To the left of the door was a BBQ area, well, let's say a mini kitchen area with a stainless-steel BBQ the size of a tank. Well, a small car anyway. Joe headed towards the table and pulled a seat out for me and one for himself, then sat down. Joe said rather sternly, "I have one rule, Will, no smoking in the house please, even though I smoke myself, I don't like the yellow it does to the walls and ceilings."

"No problem at all, Joe," I said, all the while thinking to myself that it was not like England; it's ok to stand outside and smoke, no rain either. We sat for about twenty minutes, enjoying the evening and smoking a few cigarettes before Joe said, "I'm going to take a shower and jump into bed. It's been a very long week for me, Will. I hope you don't think I'm a terrible host."

"Not at all, Joe," I said. "I think you're great. Not many people would allow a stranger to stay at their house."

"Just don't rob me," he laughed.

"I'm out in the morning tomorrow Will, I have a little work to do first thing, but I should be back by around lunchtime. Help yourself to any food, beers, and there's a coffee machine in there, but Cameron is the only one who knows how to use it." As he lifted the lid on the outside bin and put his empty bottle in, he turns back to look at me and smiled, spreading out his hands. "Mi casa es su casa," he said, then laughed. "My house is your house; you'll learn with time. Night Will."

I bid him goodnight and thanked him once again for being so kind to a complete stranger. Maybe if more people were like him, this world would be a better place.

I didn't see or even hear Joe again that night. I drank one more beer, smoked a couple more cigarettes, and decided to call it a night.

I closed the patio door and turned the light off. I gingerly walked towards my room to keep the noise down. I grabbed my backpack from the front door then headed into my room. The clock on the nightstand said 11.02 pm. I have now been awake longer than 24 hours. I pushed the door closed, stripped my clothes off down to my boxer shorts, and fell forward, face first, onto the bed. This has been a hell of a long twenty-four hours. I was gone in seconds after my head hit that pillow; my mind and body shut down simultaneously as I drifted off, feeling content.

3

JOE DICORPO & CAMERON REILLY

I woke to find the sun was already peeking around the curtains; I was a little disorientated when my eyes first opened. I did not recognise my surroundings, and for a split second, I panicked until my mind realised where I was. I stretched my whole body out in the bed and yawned loudly. I looked towards the alarm clock on the bedside table; it read 9.12 am. I groaned and slid my body to the edge of the bed, to will myself to get up. After a couple of seconds, I got to my feet. It was then that the excitement came over me. I had made it. I'm in California.

I went to the restroom, as we all do in the morning. I could murder a cuppa. I pulled the bedroom curtains open to let the sunshine in and was blinded immediately through the glass doors. I focused my eyes on the view, which had been difficult to see the previous evening in the night sky. There were mountains, well, big hills at least, as far as my eyes could see. I turned to search for my backpack. I dropped inside the door the night before and emptied the contents of the main section to the floor.

Shorts, where are my shorts?

I searched through the pile. I gasped and then smiled to myself. There you are, my Everton shorts. Everton had been the football team I picked out of the two teams to support in

Liverpool. Mostly, because I liked the colour blue more than the colour red, funny how the mind's of children work. I slipped them on, grabbed my cigarettes off the bedside cabinet, and opened the bedroom door. I headed out confident that I was indeed alone. The house was empty. However, I'm sure I heard Joe pop his head around the bedroom door, saying that he would see me later this morning. At least I think I heard him.

As I walked towards the kitchen, I remember what Joe had said about the coffee machine and that his friend Cameron was the only one who knew how to use it. I figured there had to be tea bags in one of these cupboards as I'd now reached the doorway of the kitchen. I went on a fruitless search, looking in drawers, cupboards, jars, and containers. I couldn't find anything except coffee beans, but I had no idea how to turn this into morning java. There was not a jar of instant coffee anywhere in sight. I chuckled as I opened the fridge and pulled out a Coors Light.

"Oh well, 9.30 wake up beer it is," I spoke out loud to myself. "It would be rude not to." As I exited the kitchen doorway, I took a small sip just too wet my throat, opened the patio doors, and stepped out into a heat I've never felt before. I took one step, then immediately jumped back inside the patio door. "Hell no," I said and laughed to myself. The patio floor was hot enough to fry an egg on and so impossible to walk barefoot on.

I rushed back to my room, and after a quick search, retrieved my trainers; I had kicked off last night as I fell into bed. I slipped them on and exited the bedroom, which was already heating up since I had drawn the curtains back some minutes earlier. I walked across the hall, and I went back through the glass doors.

Beer in one hand, cigarettes in the other, I headed for the table that I'd sat at last night with Joe and immediately put the umbrella up that was coming up through a hole in the centre of the table. I wasn't ready for this heat difference, which will take some getting used to. Well, at least until my body manages to acclimatise to these conditions. I sat down on the seat I had sat in the previous evening and lit up a smoke. Now was the first time I could look at my surroundings. I lifted my hand to block the sun from blinding my view. For as far as my eyes could see, it was hills and mountains, on which trees and bushes were growing wild. The terrain looked very rough, with a lot of sand and stones and boulders. To the far left, I could make out the outlines of tall buildings, possibly the downtown area of Los Angeles' skyscrapers. It appeared to be all hazy. I looked around for the few lights I had seen the night before dotted in the surrounding hills and could hardly make out the houses in the distance. Was this living the dream? If it wasn't, then it was damn close. I laughed to myself and sipped at my chilled beer.

I'd drank a few beers by lunchtime when Joe came in. "Beer, Will?" he asked in a questioning voice from the patio doors. "Yeah, please, Joe," I shouted toward him as he slipped back in the doorway, just out of sight.

I heard the front door shut, and then a female voice shouted. "WHERE YOU AT MY STUD MUFFIN?" I smirked to myself at this.

I heard Joe respond, "Oh Cameron, I've missed you." I listened to the muffled sounds of them greeting each other in the hallway.

Sounding breathless, she asked Joe, "how hot was home?" and "was the flight, ok?"

Joe responded, "What are you drinking, we can go out back, and I'll tell you all about it."

The voice quickly responded. "I'm having the same as you, duh Joe," and she gave out a small chuckle.

"Come meet my new English buddy, he's out back," Joe said as he moved into view. The female voice I heard just now also came into view. The first thing to catch my eye was how small she was compared to Joe.

She looked at me as she walked towards the table and said, "hi, I'm Cam, sorry Cameron, but just call me Cam, everyone else does." As she got closer, I raised myself out of my seat to greet her. She had blonde hair tied up in a ponytail. She was very petite and slender, but it was clear to me she works out. She was wearing a pair of Demin shorts, the type that you buy already frayed on and around the edges, an orange tank top, and you could glimpse the straps of the blue bikini top she wore underneath tied around her neck. A white pair of flick off sandals made her feet look tiny. Her voice sounded welcoming, and the look in her piercing blue eyes was overwhelmingly inviting. You don't see the type of genuine look often, but you recognise it when you see it. She leaned in to give me a small hug, and as she did, the sweet aroma of her perfume filled the air and lingered for a few seconds.

I responded, "Alright Cam, nice to meet ya. I'm Will."

"Oh my," she responded, giving me a little smile, then turned to Joe and said, "The women are going to go nuts over that accent, and he's not half bad looking either." Joe handed me my beer, to which I smiled. Joe smiled back and then towards Cameron, whom he shrugged his shoulders as if to say *how would he know.*

We sat around for quite a while, just talking and learning about each other. I wasn't always entirely forthcoming about my past. I told stories that had half-truths and a few that were fabricated to make myself look more amusing and fun to be around. I preferred to hear about their lives. I knew mine and that I didn't have much to talk about. I heard how Cameron and Joe had both grown up in San Antonio, and that's how their families had met.

Joe was twenty-eight, so I was right; he was a few years older than me. He had only had his birthday the previous month, and to hear him describe it was rather amusing. He told me about all the people who had come, particularly the women, and even compared it to the playboy mansion. Cameron laughed at this and said, "Joe is always horny, he's constantly thinking with the wrong head," and laughed again.

Joe smirked as if he was proud of this title and then responded, "you only live once, Cam." Joe's family owned one of the largest beverage supplying companies in the states. His grandfather had come over from Maglie in Italy in 1912 at the young age of 19 to avoid being drafted into the First World War. Joe's family had been in the town of Maglie for as long as history told. His grandfather had worked his way across on a cotton boat coming up from the cape of Africa. He had started out selling cola drinks in glass bottles on the street corners of San Antonio, Texas, which had now grown into a multimillion-dollar industry. Joe's father, Tony, who runs the company now that their grandfather has passed away, had changed the business plans in the sixties to include alcoholic beverages. They now are the biggest suppliers of beer, wine, and spirits to half the grocery store chains in the United States.

Joe is the younger of two brothers. His older brother Johnny had gone on to become a paediatric doctor in Cedars-Sinai. Ceder-Sinai is one of, if not the top, paediatric hospitals in America. To hear him describe his older brother as "the Blue eye of the family" was rather quite amusing to me sitting in a huge house in the mountains. Joe came out to California for university and graduated with a business management degree. Joe had become accustomed to the life in California because it was a lot more hustle and bustle, which is precisely what he liked, so he stayed afterwards. He went to work for his father Tony in the family business and now handles the west coast accounts. The house he's living in and the place I'm currently staying was bought for him by his parents after he graduated to give him a start in life. "Nice start," I said once he told me this and laughed.

Cameron sat down and let Joe talk. She was more tightly lipped than Joe, and it was difficult for me to see inside her. Once the vodka started flowing, Cameron's lips loosened up, and she began to talk about her life. Cameron, who was 23 years old, had graduated from San Antonio University and received honour grades in business and law. Her father and mother had started one of the world's finest holiday homes. I'm not talking like a Butlins Hi-de Hi type of place, more along the likes of private yachts and golden villas, those platinum service retreats that cater exclusively for the rich and famous. I heard how many people in the world drop fifty thousand dollars on a weekend break. I sat there thinking about that as they carried on talking. Fifty thousand thrown away on a weekend, the thought baffled me. I was lucky to have fifty pounds to my name.

Cameron, didn't want to work so her parents give her a monthly allowance to live on. She was 'young and enjoying life', to quote her own words. Cameron had lost her brother, Darren, two years back, and she was having difficulties dealing with this. In an attempt to help her parents had sent her out to visit Joe in California after she had started to go off the rails in San Antonio. Cameron became accustomed to the lifestyle and decided to stay. Joe and Cameron's brother Darren had been best friends all their lives. They went to the same schools together, then college, and then on to university. Darren and Joe had first met in high school at the age of 12 when they both joined the school baseball team. Darren carried on with baseball at university, and according to the two of them, he was good enough to turn professional. They both moved out to California for university because Darren had convinced Joe to go to UCLA. Darren had been out drinking with a friend one night and was killed in a drink driving incident. His friend was at fault for being three times over the legal limit. Cameron said he got five years for vehicular manslaughter. It was clear from her tone she didn't feel this was near long enough. Joe looked towards Cameron with sympathy in his eyes and face. They have become already close joined at the hip and had comforted each other at the time of Darren's death and the trial that followed. They created a bond that was unbreakable by anything or anyone. Cameron sometimes looked at Joe as if he was Darren and Joe adored Cameron, just like his baby sister.

We spent most of the night drinking and chatting. I could see just how nice these two were, and deep down, they were very sincere people. As the night went on, it felt as if I had known them both for years.

• • •

During the daytime, over the next two weeks, Cameron would take me places. Mostly the beach to sunbathe, as this is what I enjoyed doing the most. She took me to loads of different sightseeing spots. We spent a whole day walking around Sunset Blvd, searching for stars' names on the sidewalk. Cameron's favourite was Marilyn Monroe's star. I saw stars for miles; they didn't just go down one road; they went around loads of different avenues.

I visited the handprints and footprints in Mann's Chinese theatre. Cameron took me into Fredrick's of Hollywood in actual Hollywood. Every woman that worked there was stunning. She embarrassed me by asking if I could model for her a pair of leather thongs. I even had a photograph taken with me standing to the side of the incredible hulk outside the wax museum.

We walked up and down rodeo drive and laughed at how the other half lived. I saw gold watches on display for $200,000. I saw a man's tailor's shop, and Cameron told me that's where George Bush Jr. and Bill Clinton get their suits. "100,000 a suit," Cameron told me. This not only amazed but baffled me at how there was that much money in the world.

We drove all around Beverly Hills as Cameron pointed out celebrity's places. I couldn't believe the sizes of these homes. The last place Cameron showed me was the mayor of Beverly Hills' private mansion. This had its own road and was the only mansion on the street. We sat on some sandy road for two hours, talking with each other as I sunbathed and looked towards the huge Hollywood sign.

Cameron took me to Venice beach to walk up and down the beachfront and go in and out of the stalls. I knew this wasn't for her because she had a scrunched up face when I initially suggested it. I understand now why Cameron had been reluctant to take me there. It was full of run-down people, and the homeless had set up there. Before long, the city of Venice beach was full of vagrants. I thought if it wasn't for meeting Joe at the airport, this could have been me. I looked towards a man in his late 60s, wearing only one shoe, his trousers were ripped and dirty, his shirt three times bigger than his body.

Cameron took me to places I'd never heard of before. We walked up and down the pier in Santa Monica. We sat at the end and had lunch in a sandwich bar. Cameron even managed to get me on the waltzes ride on the way off the pier. We grabbed a Mr. Whippy ice cream as we left for the drive. I had to hold Cameron's for her to lick as she drove, as it was melting in the heat and would have gone everywhere.

There was still more of Los Angeles to see, and each day Cameron showed me something different. I had no idea how big the city of Los Angeles alone is, never mind the state itself. This wasn't like Europe, at least there, you could jump on a bus. Here everywhere we drove was 40 minutes away, and I laughed as I thought about some of the bus rides I'd taken in Europe.

As each day passed by, me and Cameron grew closer to each other and started to bond. We had learnt each other's little quirks. I knew not to bother her if she hadn't had coffee in the morning. After throwing up drunk one night, she learnt not to give me Jägermeister shots ever again. I had been to a few nightclubs during the week with Cameron when Joe had to work the next day or had gone to bed early. I dressed in clothes I'd borrowed from Joe to go out. I didn't own anything suitable myself for a nightclub.

Cameron knew a lot of people in Santa Monica and was always trying to hook me up with one of her girlfriends. Cameron looked like the typical Californian. Blonde hair, blue eyes, a beach body most women would kill for. People were drawn to her charm, charisma, and the way she held herself. She brought happiness wherever she went. She introduced me to all her girlfriends and some even tried to pass me their phone numbers. I met her best friends, Jess and Kristen. Cameron had previously warned me off; to use her words, 'don't sleep with either of them, it will only make things complicated'.

She explained how Jess and Kristen had helped her after she

first moved to Santa Monica and sheltered her from the known creeps in the nightclubs. Cameron's main club, the 555, was on First Avenue, next to the beach in Santa Monica. Cameron walked in there every time like she owned the place. The security greeted her as she entered, and they all gave her a small peck on the check. One of them went to stop me until Cameron intervened and said, "he's with me." To which he sat back in his seat. This wasn't like any nightclub I'd ever seen before. It was huge, and there were hundreds of people in there. Cameron introduced me to a man who was about her age called Roland. He was a light-skinned Hispanic, dressed in a black short-sleeved button-down collar shirt that had a logo on the front, black shoes, and light casual trousers, although it was hard to make out in the dim lights of the nightclub. I hadn't seen this logo on the shirt before. It was hard to see in the mass of people whose feet belonged to whom. His head and face were completely shaven. He was a lot smaller than me, but his shoulders matched mine in width. He said hello to me politely over the noise of the music and then leaned in to whisper in Cameron's ear and give her a little peck on the cheek. He looked at me when doing so as if he were unsure if Cameron was my partner or not, and then he disappeared into the crowd, lost in the sea of people. Seconds later, Cameron grabbed me by the arm, and I could see she was all excited.

"He's gorgeous, don't you think, Will?"

I laughed, as it was obvious from Cameron's face that she liked this, Roland. I laughed at Cameron but also thought how cute she was at the same time. "Let's grab a drink, Cam," I said.

Cameron had dated a few guys in California, but she had said earlier in the week how she thought guys her own age weren't ready for a serious relationship. They were too busy out playing boy racers in their cars or getting stupid drunk with their friends. I laughed at her as I smiled and said, "Wisdom comes with age."

Cameron did introduce me to Tameka, well Meka is how Cameron had initially greeted her. She was older than Cameron, maybe even a little older than me. Meka was stunning, beyond beautiful. She was a light-skinned black woman with dazzling deep brown eyes and shoulder-length curly hair. She was slender and had legs that reached up to her armpits ,she wore a black sequin dress that barely covered her midsection and matching shoes. She looked good, but Meka was the type of woman that knew this. I'm sure she couldn't pass a mirror without looking at herself. I became, well, let's just say, friends with Meka, but it was mostly when Meka wanted company. This worked well for me. I did things with Meka that made me the lover I am to this day. I had never connected intimately like this with anyone else I'd dated before. Not that Meka wanted to date. She was happy living her life, and the situation worked for us both in more ways than one. Meka had a small butterfly tattoo on her lower back. This was the first person I'd slept with that had a tattoo is the only reason I mention it.

On most of the evenings, when Joe came home from work, we would sit out on the patio and drink Coors until late in the evening. Cameron was there sometimes, but most of the time, she was out or would hang around for a few hours once Joe came home, have some food, or some days she would just cook for us. Cameron was constantly on her phone in the daytime arranging what she was doing with Jess or Kristen that evening. During my time sat alone with Joe in the evenings, I learned a lot more about him. Not just the normal everyday things we all show on the outside. I got a sense of trust when I spoke to Joe. I began to see him as a close friend. I could find myself opening up to Joe and relaxing more around him. I hadn't had any friends like this before, just a few friends I'd met casually through others or while under the influence of drugs. Joe was like me. If he said he was going to do something, he just got on and did it. Joe had given me full range to use his clothes, as we were similar in height and weight. I felt as if I was a new man. I helped around the place as much as I could. I cleaned most mornings, well, I helped Cameron clean before we would leave for the day sightseeing.

Over the next two weeks, I had grown to like both Joe and

Cameron, and for the first time, I was learning to trust someone. I heard from Cameron how she and Joe used to stay in the same house before she got her own place in Santa Monica. Joe had told me how when Cameron first came out to California, she had stayed in the house with him. How Cameron wanted to party every night and at first how Joe had gone and accompanied her, but Cameron can do that seven days a week.

"I have to work Monday to Friday, so coming home at 4 in the morning and being at work by 9 wasn't working for me. So, Cameron rents an apartment in Santa Monica and stays there whenever she goes clubbing. It works best for us both," said Joe. I lay on the bed that night drifting away and realised I was smiling to myself. I was happy, I mean really happy.

4

DARYL POINTER & ROBERT CENTRES

We turned down onto Cameron's street, Oak Avenue. I still have no idea why it was called this because there wasn't a single oak tree in sight. Instead, the sidewalk had palm trees running down the side that appeared to be reaching for the sun as they stretched upwards, so tall. Cameron's place was on the right, looking out towards the ocean. "You can see Catalina Island from my kitchen window," she told me as if I had ever heard of Catalina Island.

Cameron reached for the garage clicker and indicated to pull onto the driveway. The garage door opened as we drove inside, and once coming to a halt, she clicked the door closed. The sunlight disappeared slowly as the garage door closed until all the light that remained was coming from under the doorway to our left. We were running into Cameron's apartment quickly, so she could feed her goldfish and wait for her pot dealer Daryl to show up. Cameron laughed as I asked her if I could jump in the shower quickly at her place. It had been hotter in Griffin Park than the previous week. I spent most of my time lying on a beach sunbathing in the sea breeze.

The observatory in Griffin Park was on top of a hill in the middle of nowhere. The heat had nowhere to go because you were closer to the sun. She pushed my leg lightly and gestured her head as if to say, get out the jeep. She began to climb out the driver's side. "I'll show you where I keep the towels," she replied as she turned and headed towards the light coming from the door.

I followed Cam as she went through the door. The sunlight hit us again, and I felt the warm air race across my face. We went up the wooden stairs from the garage up to the next level. Then we walked along a small hall, and we entered the living room. On my left was the front door with windows on either side, which not only lit up the room but made it feel warmer than outside.

The room was rather large, roughly around twelve feet across by ten feet in length. On the right to the corridor we came out of, there was a huge TV mounted on the wall with a couch and coffee table halfway through the room. The couch was large, but it fitted adeptly into this room. Cameron picked up her mail, which lay below the letterbox of the front door and walked past me. "This way, Will," she said as she headed quickly towards a corridor on the left side of the building.

This appeared to be a small, dark corridor. The first door we passed was open. This was the kitchen. I had caught sight of the wooden table and chairs as we passed the doorway. There were two more doors on the left, just past the kitchen.

One of the doors was open, so I could see that this was a bedroom. The bedspread was all frilly and light pink. I followed Cameron halfway down the corridor as she opened a door on the right. "Shower," she said to me, from the doorway, with a smile on her face. "There are clean towels in that cupboard in front of you," as she pointed towards a large wall mounted white cabinet. As she squeezed past me in the doorway, I caught myself smelling her hair. I could smell the strawberry shampoo she had used in her hair that morning. "Daryl is usually on time," she said as she walked up the corridor and turned into the kitchen doorway. I closed the door. I reached in, flipped the shower on, and stripped my clothes off. I grabbed a fresh towel from the cupboard and checked the water temperature before stepping in.

As I stepped out of the shower, I could hear voices in the other room. I figured that must be the guy Cameron had been waiting on. I dried myself off with the towel, put my clothes back on, and cleaned up a little before opening the door to exit.

Once the door was open, I heard a few voices coming from what sounded like the apartment's kitchen area. The voices appeared to be raised as if someone was shouting. It sounded as if the voices shouting were in angry. I crept up the corridor unsure and nervously looked around the corner. The kitchen was empty. The raised voices were coming from the living room. I moved closer to the edge of the corridor; my heart was pounding. "What was going on". Once I reached the end, the living room it became visible. Firstly I could see a rather large black guy with his back to me. He stood about my height, but he was a lot larger than me. His clothes looked baggy on him. His black shirt was stretched out and overwashed. The black denim jeans he wore had seen better days. The heels on the legs had all frayed as if they had been dragged along the floor. Half his boxer shorts were exposed at the waistline as if he hadn't fastened his belt up tight enough, and so they had sagged down. Out of the corner of my eye, I can see Cameron being held on the couch by some other guy. This guy was hard to see as the couch partially hid him. His face was unshaven and looked to have at least three days of stubble on him. He hadn't had a haircut in quite a while because it was all jagged around the edges, left to grow wild and unattended. The guy was groping her and trying to get her clothes off. His hand slipped under her shirt, and then Cameron started crying and screaming, "Don't, please don't."

I pulled my head back around the corner. What am I going to do? I thought, my heart rate began climbing rapidly. I was very scared. No, I was fucking terrified. I rush quietly back into the bathroom. The fear lingered in the pit of my stomach. How can I help Cameron? I must help her somehow. I began panting under my breath silently. I looked to see if there is anything I could use as a weapon to defend myself. There was nothing. I couldn't find anything in there of any use. I came out of the bathroom and headed towards the next room. Opening the door quietly, I saw only a bed and dresser in this room. This must be the spare room. I proceeded towards the next door and heard a scream come from the living room from Cameron. I rushed into the room and started to look for something. I was running out of time. I found an umbrella leaning on the doorjamb behind the door. This had no weight to it. I carried on searching and came across a baseball bat at the side of the bed that had either rolled or been put under the bed. I grabbed it with both hands and headed out the door.

As I came towards the end of the corridor, I could see the shadow of a figure moving, so I slowed down. As I peered around the corner, I could see the guy on top of Cameron pulling at her shorts. The other guy said to him, "Just rip them off." I looked at him and decided he was the first one I should go for. I breathed quietly so as not to be heard and readied myself. I counted to three, but it wasn't long enough. I couldn't go out. I breathed fast as I heard Cameron pleading with the man to stop. I knew I had to go out there, but I'm more scared now than I've ever been. My heart feels as if it's going to bounce clean out of my chest; my stomach had turned into knots with fear. I can feel my leg begin to shake as my nerves were fighting to take over. A small part of my mind was saying to hide until this is all over.

Stop it; you have to try and help Cameron. Count to three again, count to three again. One, two….

I could feel my body moving, but my mind was guiding it. I rushed around the corner as fast as my legs could move. I raised the bat with both my hands. The black guy, who had been jeering the other guy on, suddenly turned towards me. As he did, I was upon him. I swung the bat with all my strength and watched as it connected with the side of his head. Now, remember this is real life, not a movie. He didn't go down. He only stumbled a little on his feet and then looked towards me with rage. I brought the bat down again and then again until I knew he was on the floor and not moving. I turned to where Cameron was. The man she was being held down by reached towards his waist and pulled out a silver gun. I'd already started towards him and was half in my swing with the bat when the gun drew up level with my chest. The gun clicked. I know what they say, at the point of death, your life flashes before eyes. I saw and felt nothing.

I brought the bat down on the shoulder of this man with all my might, which knocked him clean off Cameron and onto the floor. Am I shot? I don't feel anything? Cameron leapt over the couch the second she felt freedom. As she reared up, she came in the middle of us in any attempt to escape him. Just as I went to swing again, I tried to get out her way, but she collided with me, and my back spun round. I ended up over the coffee table and onto the floor, flat on my back. The baseball bat bounced on the floor and headed towards the kitchen doorway, far away from my grasp.

I pushed forward as if to get straight back to my feet. I saw the face of the guy I had just hit diving towards me. He landed with his full weight on my chest and punched me in the ear with his right hand. My eyes went blurry; I could feel the heat rushing into my ear as the blood rushed to that spot. He went to hit me again with his left fist. I managed to get my arm up to protect the side of my head somewhat as the punch arrived. The next thing I knew, he had somehow caught me on my chin. I felt light-headed, one more punch, and I would be gone. I looked in the eyes of this man on top of me. They only showed anger as foam appeared at the corners of his mouth, wild with rage. He drew his right arm back to hit me again. This would have been it; I was already struggling after the last punch had connected. I could feel my strength dissolving in my body, and there was nothing I could do to stop it.

Suddenly, I heard a sound of such volume that I had never heard before. It continued to echo in my ears for some time afterwards. It was a gunshot. The guy on top of me stopped, and for a split second, I wasn't sure what had just happened. He then fell off me and landed in a heap on the floor. I looked around as my ears were buzzing with the sound. My head was throbbing from the punch, but my ears hadn't yet sorted themselves out.

Cameron was standing with the gun in her hands. She was shaking but still pointing it towards this man who wasn't moving at all. Strength began to return to my body as I recovered from the punch that had nearly finished me. I managed to claw myself up the back of the couch. I turned and rushed towards where the bat had landed. I grabbed the bat off the floor and rushed towards the guy who was on top of me. His eyes were open, but he was no longer there. His eyes looked blankly right back at me. The backside of his head was gone. He was dead. I sped to the next guy who was lying face down and checked him for a pulse. Nothing, he was also dead. I stood up, and Cameron, who was still holding the gun trained on the guy, was frozen stiff in that position. I made my way towards her. "It's ok, Cam," I said as I reached to take the gun off her. She let go with no problem. I don't think she wanted to pick it up in the first place anyway. I placed the gun on the coffee table. I'd fallen over only a minute or two prior. I dropped the baseball bat to the floor and put my arms around Cameron and pulled her in close to my body. "Are you ok?" I said as she leaned on my chest and started sobbing.

"Yes," she said. "Are you ok, Will? He was hitting you, and I thought he was going to kill you."

"I'm fine; my granny hits harder than that." I chuckled nervously, trying to make light of what had just happened. I held Cameron tight in my arms. I walked her around the couch and sat her down. I sat down beside her and hugged her tighter than I've ever hugged anyone. We sat quietly as if we both had the last five minutes playing on repeat over and over again in our minds. Then it dawned on me; we have two dead bodies in the room with us. I released Cam from my hug. I pulled out my cigarettes that had become a little crushed over the previous minutes rolling around. I lit one up and put my arm around Cameron once more. We sat there for a few minutes in complete silence.

After a few minutes, Cameron said, "What are we going to do? Should I call the cops, Will?"

"No, Cameron, not yet, let me think please, Hun". I lit a second smoke off the first one before standing the old one up on the coffee table. My mind started racing. "Ok, so we call the police, and we tell them what happened, and it will be ok as they attacked you," I say to Cameron.

Cameron, who also has now had time to think, quickly responds. "No, no, Will, what will happen is the cops will come out and arrest us for murder in a drug deal gone wrong. That's the way they will see it."

"WHAT!" I replied with a sense of fear in my voice.

She jumped straight back in "the cops in this country aren't like England, Will. We will both be locked up and maybe even given the death penalty at the very least we will spend the rest of our lives in prison."

I was shocked to hear this, but to be fair, I had no faith in the court system back in the UK either, so I believed anything was possible. We sat looking at the two bodies on the floor, and I turned to Cameron and asked her. "What happened, I thought you knew him." Cameron went on to explain what had happened, and I sat and listened to every word. She told me that Daryl showed up at the door and pointed towards the black guy lying half in the hall and half in the living room. She told me how she had never seen this man before and pointed towards the guy slumped in a heap. He was with Daryl, who she'd dealt with loads of times so that he couldn't have been all that bad. Letting them in, it was then she saw Daryl's eyes. He was high on something, she explained. They came, in and his friend immediately started to try and pull her in as if he was trying to get a hold of her. She told me how she kept pushing him off. Daryl started to do the deal, but his friend wouldn't stop.

"I asked Daryl to stop him, and he didn't listen. His friend kept on pushing towards me as I was trying to back away, and he grabbed me by my arms. I couldn't stop him; he was on top of me.

He forced me down on the couch. He was too strong for me to stop. He was trying to kiss me, but I wouldn't, so he tried grabbing me, then I started to really panic," she said, trembling. "I knew he wasn't going to stop." She started crying but continued her story. "He was going to rape me. Then you came running out. I saw him reaching for a gun. I was trying my hardest to fight back. I had grabbed his wrist twice and stopped him. When you hit the guy, he dropped the gun. I jumped off the couch as quick as I could and rushed for it before he got up again. As soon as he did, he jumped towards you and kept on hitting you. So I shot him," she finished.

She went on to thank me repeatedly. I didn't say how scared I was, but I told her what I had seen and my version of what had happened. I could feel my heart rate slowly coming down, I wasn't breathing heavy any longer.

"I thought he was going to shoot you. When he pulled the trigger, he didn't realise the safety was still on the gun. We are lucky to be alive, Will. We really are."As she wiped her eyes again with her hand.

I know Cameron trusted Joe with her life, but could I. Now I'm going to have to, also. I can't clean this up alone, and Cam isn't mentally or physically strong enough. I told Cameron, 'I'm calling Joe and having him meet us here'. At first, she didn't want me to, as it would upset him. I explained that it was way past that point. I told her we no longer have a choice and explained we have to get rid of the bodies. She can't lift with me, and I can't do it alone. Although she insisted she was strong enough to help, she understood the point I was making. Cameron stood up and walked to the phone, and brought it over to me.

"Press two and call. He's saved in the phone."

I lit another cigarette as Cameron went out to the kitchen and called Joe. Cameron came back in the room with an ashtray as the phone rang and started cleaning up my previously smoked butts. It was only then I had realised and said, "Sorry, Cam. I didn't even ask if it's ok to smoke in here."

As I finished, Joe picked up the other end of the line. "Hello, Joe Dicorpos," he said in a very clear voice.

"Hey Joe, it's Will. Can you talk quickly?"

"Yeah, no problem, bud. What's going on?"

I wanted to scream down the phone what had happened. Joe was my friend, someone who had opened his home to me, someone who treated me like a brother. I knew, I just couldn't. I asked him if he could head over to Cameron's after finishing work as she is cooking pasta.

"Yeah, no problem. I'm on my way in five. That girl can cook."

"Ok. No problem, see you soon."

I hung up with Joe and passed the phone to Cameron.

"Thanks, Hun."

As she stood up to put it back, my mind remembered something. "Did you feed the goldfish?" Why this came to mind now, I have no idea.

"Yes, I did, as soon as we arrived." She replied

We sat together, leaning our bodies on each other on the couch for about 30 minutes. If we talked, I don't remember anything we said. My mind was spinning.

I heard the garage door open and close after Joe had driven in. I told Cameron to trust me because I had an idea. I was going to keep Joe's eyes closed until he got in the kitchen. Then I could sit him down and explain what had happened. Joe walked towards me up the stairs and asked how I was. I told him I was fine.

"How did you like the observatory, bud?" he asked as he neared the top of the stairs.

"It was too hot," I said to Joe. "I need you to do me a favour close your eyes tight for me. There is something in the living room I can't show you just yet." And smiled, he looked at me all intrigued.

"I like surprises," he chuckled as he reached the top of the stairs.

We all like surprises, but this isn't anything nice to look forward to.

"Close your eyes, Joe, tight now mind. No peeking, I'll guide you." I replied as I grabbed his arm, and he closed his eyes. I motioned him forward by pulling lightly on his arm and manoeuvred him around the coffee table, which was still off skew since I fell backwards over it. As we passed the two bodies on the floor, I said, "No spying Joe, that's cheating." As soon as we had passed the kitchen doorway, I told Joe that it was ok to open his eyes. I released his arm as I no longer needed to guide him.

"What's going on?" said Joe with a smile on his face.

Cameron said, "Have a seat, Joe. We have something we need to talk to you about." Joe sat at the kitchen table as I passed him a Coors light out of the fridge.

Cameron went first and explained what had happened, and Joe looked at her in total disbelief. "Will, what's going on?" he directed towards me with concern. I explained my side of the events, and Joe looked white. "So they are in the living room?" Joe asked. "I want to see them," he said in a demanding tone.

"Come on then," I said quietly as I walked through the doorway and back into the living room. Joe followed me, but Cameron stayed in the kitchen. Joe stood just inside the living room and looked at the carnage. After a few seconds had passed.

"What the fuck are we going to do, Will?" he said with a sense of fear in his voice.

"It's ok, Joe, don't worry, we can sort this out," I said as he lifted the bottle to his lips and took a sip of the beer. "Cameron, I wonder, do you have a pen and some paper, please?" with a slightly raised voice to make sure she could hear me in the kitchen.

"Yeah, of course, Will," she responded. "There's paper and a pen in the drawer here." Me and Joe headed back towards the kitchen. Joe sat down right away, and Cameron stood at the kitchen sink looking towards us as I sat down in the seat across from Joe again.

"I'm scared," she said. "The cops will throw us in jail." You could hear the panicked tone in her voice.

"It's ok, Cam, don't worry," I said to her. "I can fix this, but I'm going to need both of you to help. I can't do it alone. We need to trust each other and work together to solve this." They both looked towards each other then back to me.

Joe replied, "We do trust you, Will. What do you need us to do?"

"Cameron, can I have the paper and pen please, I need to make a list." Cameron went in the drawer next to the cooker and pulled out a notepad and pen, and placed it in front of me on the table. I began to make my list of what I figured we would need to dispose of these two without leaving any trace. I wasn't sure were yet but I knew we had to get rid of their bodies. Black bags, rolls of them, sheets of plastic, a shovel; my list was growing fast. My brain began racing. "What if someone heard the gunshot?" I said out loud, without realising I had spoken.

Cameron responded, "if someone heard the shot, the cops would already be here by now. The cops don't come out to every gunshot call" She paused then and followed with, "It's been over an hour since the shooting, so if they were coming, they would be here by now." I leaned back in my seat, relieved with the fact the police weren't coming. My list grew and grew as we sat there for most of the night in the kitchen.

Finally, I said, "Ok, I have got this; you both need to do exactly what I say so we can walk away from this unscathed."

I looked at both of them and said, "It's getting on now. We will need to sleep soon. Cameron grabbed a black bag". We watched as she reached into the cupboard under the sink for the roll.

"I need you to go in the shower, take off all your clothes, and put them straight into the black bag. Get in, wash your hair, scrub every inch of your body. When you're finished, get dried off, put the towels in the black bag, and don't touch the black bag again. When you're done, go to your room and get dressed." I smiled, but she knew I was serious about the matter-of-fact way I had delivered the instructions. "Ready for another beer?" I asked Joe as I got up and walked towards the fridge.

"Please," he said as Cameron headed towards the door.

"I'll see you in a few minutes," she said. Both Joe and I smiled towards her as she went through the doorway. As I scribbling things down on my list when they came into my mind, Joe sat quietly with a fearful look on his face. He smoked a cigarette, and as I was writing on the pad, I could see in his face he had now realised fully the extent of the situation we were in.

"It's ok, Joe," I said. "Don't worry. We can sort this out."

Joe sent a half-smile my way and said, "I hope so, Will. I can't lose Cam. She isn't strong enough to make it in jail. She's still very fragile after Darren's death." I stood up from the table and pulled his arm, forcing him to stand up. I put my arms around him and hugged him.

"Don't worry; she's going nowhere. I've got this, Joe." As I released him from the hug, we both sat down in our seats again on either side of the table.

Then, from nowhere, as Cameron was now approaching the kitchen, Joe said, "I'll have to call my father and take the rest of the week off." I didn't respond to this. I didn't even look up from my notepad. Cameron entered the room.

"I think I've done exactly what you said, Will," said Cameron as she adjusted the towel she had rolled up like a turban on her head. "Perfect, Cam, I'll get in myself just before bed. It was then that Cameron realised she only had two beds.

"One of you will have to sleep in my room with me," she said. "I only have two bedrooms."

Joe responded right away before I had fully absorbed what she had said. "Will and I can share the same bed, is that ok, Will? I nodded at them both. Joe and Cameron continued talking for a little before Joe retired to the bedroom. Cameron followed almost immediately, going to her room.

I stepped into the bathroom and clicked the light on. I sat down on the edge of the bathtub for what seemed like hours, just replaying all the events that had happened. I reached over and flicked the shower on. The water came rushing out, which startled me slightly. My nerves were shot. I stood up to avoid the shower spray and undressed. I opened the cupboard once more and pulled another towel off the shelf. I draped it over the sink and stepped into the shower. Once the warm water started to cascade down my body, my mind was racing, as if it was trying to find all the answers at once. I scrubbed myself from top to bottom and then got out. I dried myself and then placed the towel into the bag Cameron had left behind the door. I tied the bag up before heading out of the room. As I turned the light off in the bathroom, everything went completely black. I felt my way into the bedroom door once my eyes had adjusted to the darkness. I could see Joe was lying on the left side of the bed, so I quietly went towards the right side so as not to wake him up. I pulled the duvet back and climbed in. As I put my head on the pillow, I remember feeling how cold the cotton felt before sleep claimed me. I was gone as if a light had been turned off.

5

CLEAN UP

The following morning, I woke up, and Joe was still asleep. I slide out of the bed so as not to wake him. The sun was coming through a small opening in the curtains that hadn't been fully closed the night before. I grabbed my t-shirt, headed towards the bedroom door while glancing at the clock on the bedside table, which read 7.32 am.

As I reached the door and began to turn the handle, Joe woke up and said, "Morning Will, you don't half snore," and laughed quietly.

"Sorry mate, I sleep like a baby," I said in response. I opened the bedroom door and informed Joe I would make him a brew.

I left the room and closed the bedroom door, just as Joe was yawning with his whole body stretched out. I looked up, and Cameron's bedroom door was already open. I headed toward the kitchen and could see that someone had draped a sheet over one of the bodies and a duvet over the other. I went through the kitchen door, and Cameron was sitting at the table in her pyjamas.

"Morning Hun, how did you sleep?" I asked, but I could see it on her face she hadn't slept well.

"Ok, I guess, all things considered," she sighed.

Joe pushed in beside me and said, "Coffee, please, Cam,"

smiling at Cameron. We sat and drank our coffee and chatted about anything we could think about other than what was in the other room waiting for us. Neither of us wanted to address the obvious fate we had in store.

After my second cup of coffee and a few cigarettes to wake up my lungs, I said, "shall we begin," and looked towards Joe and Cameron together.

Cameron announced, "Ready." Joe nodded his head. I pushed the notepad forward across the table.

"I've made a list of things we are going to need; who is to buy what, when to get it, and how much. We need to follow this list to the exact letter, or this won't work."

I showed them both my list; they read through it together. I flipped the pages of the notepad back over till I found the list again.

Scissors heavy-duty - Joe
Black bags – Cameron, grocery store
Roll of plastic sheeting - Will, hardware store
Five rolls of Duct tape - Will, hardware store
Two shovels and a pickaxe - Joe
Baby wipes ten packs - Cameron
Paper towels - Cameron
Bleach 4 bottles - Cameron
Dishwashing soap, two bottles Cameron
Rubber gloves xl four pairs, Cameron

Once they both looked over the list, Joe said, "Most of this stuff I already have in my house. I don't have plastic sheeting or duct tape. I've no use for baby wipes, but everything else is in my garage—even the shovels and pickaxe. So, we can go to home depot for the rest; it's a huge hardware store that sells everything. Oh, and I've no rubber gloves, but Cameron can grab those from anywhere."

"Perfect, Joe. Shall we make a move? Cameron, can you get the rubber gloves and meet us back here?" She looked my way with a blank stare on her face.

"Can't I just meet you at Joe's? I don't want to come back here alone," she half screamed out.

"Yeah, yeah, of course, Cam," I say with a sympathetic smile. We left the apartment at the same time and drove to the end of the road together before Cameron turned left and Joe and I turned right.

We went to home depot; it's the same as a B&Q back home, but on a larger scale. We got everything we needed, and as we headed towards the register area, we walked past the painting section. I spotted white suits, what a painter would put on with a hood over his head to spray a room as a way to protect his clothes underneath. I grabbed five and put them on the cart. We headed to pay, and before long, we were pulling into Joe's place. Cameron's car was already in front of the door as we pulled up the hill.

We got out and went in; Cameron was just out back. The patio doors were open. I walked behind Joe to the back patio, and we found Cameron sitting at the table.

"You ok?" he asks Cameron, rubbing a hand over the back of his neck.

"Yeah, I'm fine," she says.

I looked out at the hills and up at the baking sun. It was then I realised. We can bury them here. I turn to Joe and Cameron and say, "Let's drag them down to the bottom of this canyon; we can dig holes and bury them there; no one will ever find them, and no one will see us. We can dig the holes today and bring the bodies here after dark to bury them. It's perfect," I try to convince them.

Joe and Cameron look at each other than back towards me. "Ok, Will, I know a way down to the bottom, smiled Joe. Let's get the shovels." We got two shovels and a pickaxe and headed out the back.

Wringing her hands together, Cameron looked unsure of the whole situation. "I'll make us some sandwiches and bring them down after." We smiled and took off. Joe led the way down the rough terrain. I knew it wouldn't be easy to get the two of them down here. We walked down the side of the mountain for about 200 meters until we came to a slightly flattened area.

"This is perfect. We can dig here and not be seen by anyone" because there were trees covering us. I put the shovel in the ground and commenced digging. Joe moved over to my right about 8ft and started digging.

After about two hours of digging, we stopped and had lunch. Before continuing. Looking down into the hole, I could see we were about halfway, and another few feet would do it. The ground had become tougher once we got past the initial sand. We carried on digging, as we knew we had to get this done as quickly as possible. Once I got to nearly 5ft, I asked Joe how he was getting on. He had been a lot neater than me digging, that's for sure. Joe had four walls; mine was just a round hole.

We made our way back up the hill and into Joe's garden again. Cameron was lying on the lounger, sunbathing. Maybe it was the heat, maybe the fact I was exhausted from digging, I don't know, but I looked at Cameron. I mean, I looked at her this time. I was absorbing every shape that made her smooth body. Stop it, I thought, a little disappointed in myself. I should not be looking at her this way. Joe broke my train of thought suddenly. "I'm going to grab a quick shower, and we can go, Will?"

"Yeah, Joe, I'll wait until tonight. I'll grab a cold one while you shower," and smiled at him. Joe headed to the shower. I grabbed Cameron a beer, got one for myself, and sat down admiring the sunny afternoon.

After a while, we all loaded into Joe's car and headed over to the apartment. When we arrived and went into the living room, it was like we hadn't even left. Both Daryl and his friend lay there as we had left them. For a split second, I thought, as we entered the living room, that it had all been a bad dream.

I told Joe and Cameron I would do the next part alone, to leave little to no evidence if their bodies were ever discovered. Cameron looked at me with relief, as if she had been dreading this part. "Joe, can you unload everything out of the trunk of the car and bring it up here? Cameron, Hun, any chance you can grab me a beer and the black bags?"

Joe was back in a few seconds with the painter's suits and a roll of sheeting. He left and proceeded down the stairs towards the garage again. I put one of the painter's suits on, with rubber gloves on my hands, and zipped it right up to the top of the neck. I pulled the hood up. I looked as if I was an Eskimo in the Antarctic. Only my eyes were left uncovered. I took the beer off Cameron along with the roll of black bags and watched her sit down in the middle of the couch to watch.

I began to clean up. I started first with Daryl. Even though Daryl had blood coming from his head, it was nothing compared to the mess his friend had made. I put a black bag over his head to stop any excess blood dripping or splashing around. *This was already going to be difficult to clean up without adding to the mess,* the thought raced through my mind. I rolled him over, flat on his back. I asked Joe, who had unloaded the car and sat next to Cameron on the couch, to pass me the scissors. As he did, I began cutting all Daryl's clothes off piece by piece. As I cut each item of clothing off, I searched it. In the back pocket of his jeans, I found his wallet. His identification said he was Daryl Pointer and was 34 years old. I counted the money quickly and dropped it on the coffee table: fifty-two dollars. He had two plastic bags on him, one in each front pocket of his jeans. Both contained roughly an ounce of cannabis each.

When Daryl was completely naked with only the bag left on his head, I passed the scissors to Joe and asked him to cut a piece of plastic sheeting 8ft by 8ft if he could, and Cameron if she could pass me the baby wipes and kitchen towels.

I cleaned Daryl's body from top to bottom as best I could, soaking up most of the blood with paper towels. Everything I used, I put straight into a black bag. When the bag was full, Joe had my next one ready and would seal the full ones. Once Daryl lay there naked, I took the baby wipes and cleaned his whole body. Not to remove blood, just any trace of Cameron or myself. Once I was fully confident he was clean, I asked Joe to roll out the plastic sheeting he had just cut. Joe spread the sheet out next to Daryl's naked body. I rolled him over onto the plastic sheeting and began folding the edges and duct taping them closed. I did this until I was fully confident that Daryl's body was sealed. It might not be airtight, but it was damn close. "Joe, can you cut another piece of plastic sheeting 8x8, please?" I asked him. As I lifted the duvet from Daryl's friend and scrunched it into a blag bag. I grabbed another bag off the roll, lifted his head, and placed a black bag over it. The blood was dripping everywhere.

I had gotten Joe to push the paper towels underneath his head to soak up as much blood as possible. Like I had just done with Daryl, I began to cut his clothes off, putting each piece right into a black bag. When I got to his jeans, I pulled his wallet out of his pocket and opened it up. It had a few dollars in it, not much, though. His driving licence showed his face all clean-shaven and looking a lot better than he did now. Robert Centers, it said on the driving licence, 33 years old. I put the wallet in the black bag. In the front pocket were some car keys, I dropped them on the coffee table.

As soon as he was naked, Joe tied up the black bags and moved them to the garage, all ready to go. I cleaned him up just like I had done twenty minutes earlier to Daryl. I asked Cameron to pass me the gun that she had put on the top of the fridge the previous night. She walked over to the kitchen and grabbed it. I asked her if she could unload it; she did this for me then passed me the gun and bullets. I began cleaning the gun with the baby wipes. I had to make sure no fingerprints remained. I put the gun in a black bag and placed it in plastic with him. I then rolled him onto the plastic. I folded the edges and sealed them with duct tape. That was the two of them, all wrapped up and ready to go. I set to clean up the blood off the floor first, then moved to the walls and searched for any blood splatters.

Once I was satisfied I had got all the blood cleaned up, I said, "Ok, that's the hard work done." I stood up and started removing my white painter's suit, which was no longer white. I took it off along with the rubber gloves and placed them right inside another black bag that Joe had just passed me. We then lined the car trunk in plastic. We took Daryl first and struggled to get him out once we got to Joe's place as he weighed so much. We then went back for his friend. We grabbed all the black bags and everything else, as in duct tape, extra plastic, and did another clean up the last trip back.

We got back to Joe's at 11.30ish, and I was already exhausted from the day. However, we still had to get them down the hill. Cameron grabbed us all a vodka and coke and started food. We sat, drank, and ate food. At around 1.30 am, we decided it was time to get them down the hill.

We started with Daryl, as he was the larger of the two. We struggled to get him from the garage to the back patio, but it was all downhill after that. Daryl's weight did most of the work on the way down itself. We had just to guide it and not let it go too fast. We got him down to the bottom and laid him by the side of the hole. We made our way to the top and stopping to have a beer en route. I asked Cameron to follow us down this next time as we needed the black bags and scissors. She smiled and went to get things ready. We drank our beer, and Joe passed me another, which we also drank, and then we grabbed Robert, who was a lot lighter than Daryl. He was somewhat considerably easier to get to the bottom. When we got to the bottom, I cut the plastic off Robert and pushed him in the hole. I then took the plastic bag with the clean gun in it and emptied it into the hole with Robert. I did the same with Daryl. Next, I put the plastic bag, along with the plastic sheeting, in a black bag and passed the scissors to Cameron, along with the black bag. She tied the bags closed and set off up the hill. Before long, the darkness had swallowed her, and I couldn't see her anymore. I reached for my shovel and started back, filling the hole in. I said a few words for Robert as the soil covered his face. I didn't wish him to rest in peace. I somewhat saw him going the other way, as in down, for what he was trying to do to Cameron. However, I believed it was the right thing to do. Joe and I didn't talk much as we filled the holes in. We stopped now and then and had a smoke.

After what seemed the whole night, we finished filling in both holes and levelled the ground. We made our way to the top, and Cameron was sitting on a chair as we got there. She grabbed the shovels from our hands and leaned over to pass us both a beer she had sitting on the ground awaiting our return. We walked over and sat at the table.

"I'm glad that's…" started Joe.

I cut him short. "The car they came in we will get rid of later on today." We finished our beers and headed inside. I headed to the shower.

I stood in the shower for what seemed like an hour, most of the time just standing there as the water bounced off my chest. I tried to process everything that had happened in the last thirty-six hours. I played it over and over in my mind, fearful just in case I missed anything that would lead to our capture. I did the best I could think of; there's no way anyone can figure this out; I tried to convince myself. I have covered everything. I turned the shower off and dried myself, throwing some boxer shorts on and then dropping onto the bed. I caught myself thinking about Cameron again right before I drifted into unconsciousness.

I woke up at 2 pm the next day, and both Joe and Cameron were already awake. Joe was keen to get the car finished as he thought this would bring an end to all of this. I had a coffee that Cameron had made me, "Folgers," she said as she passed me the cup. "The best part of waking up is Folgers in your cup." I'm sure she had just sung me the words of some coffee commercial jingle. We sat talking, and I explained how it would be best if Cameron were to get rid of the apartment she had in Santa Monica right after we clean it out, paint the living room, and replace the carpet. It was essential that she separate herself from that place. Quickly she understood what my train of thought was, as did Joe. She laughed loudly before turning to Joe and saying, "See, I knew you couldn't get rid of me. You missed me, didn't you."

She smiled as Joe grinned back at her and said, "Of course I miss you. I get way too much sleep now you're not around." He laughed loudly to himself.

The car was easy to get rid of; we had Cameron drive it down to a deserted road off Mulholland drive. We doused it in gasoline inside and out, and I lit a match. The black bags I slowly burnt in Joe's back garden the rest of the stuff while he was at work each day until it was all gone. The baseball bat seemed to burn forever. Cameron and I cleaned out her place. She sold the furniture, most of it from the garage, over the weekend. Anything left we gave to the YMCA, who came and collected everything. We removed the carpet, and between Cameron and me, we did a half-decent job of painting the place. Cameron gave her notice, and that was the last time I ever went near the place again. Cameron moved back into Joe's place. The dynamics of the house had changed since Joe and Cameron lived together before. Now I lived there also. I became a great mediator between the two of them, who sometimes fought like brother and sister. We would talk about Daryl and Robert sometimes, but we always referred to it as the Santa Monica thing. We never used their names ever after that night. Never again.

Both Christmas and the New Year came and went. Before I knew it, three months had flown by, then six months. I was working for Joe, mainly around the place, with a bit of gardening work and cleaning the windows. I was helping Cameron with pretty much anything she asked me to do. One night Cameron decided to run to the store to grab some cigarettes, so I offered to go with her for company. On the way back home from the store, Cameron noticed a police car behind the jeep. He put his lights on as Cameron pulled to the side of the road into a lay-by to leave the road. We had just been talking about having a dinner party so that

Cameron could invite her friend Jill over. Jill was someone Cameron had met in a nightclub, and she thought we might hit it off. We had already spoken a few times. The fact she couldn't understand anything I said wasn't working for me. I was constantly repeating myself whenever I was around her. She was, however, a very nice-looking woman. As the cop approached the side of Cameron's Jeep, the cop asked to see Cameron's driving licence and proof of insurance. He said she was speeding. I said, "no way." Two words. Just "no way" from the passenger seat. The cop had me out of the jeep and in handcuffs in seconds. He wanted my identification and started searching my pockets. I looked at the once dark canyons, which had now been lit up by the blue flashing sirens of the cop car. I explained to him I only had my passport, and he started calling me an illegal alien. Cameron calmed the situation down and explained I was here on vacation, and apologised to the officer, saying I wasn't used to the sun and had a few beers earlier, which had gone right to my head. Before I knew it, I was out of cuffs, and Cameron was told to slow it down.

I sat in the seat of the jeep, looking into the night for the rest of the journey back home. As we arrived home, Cameron asked me if I was ok. I told her I was as I climbed out of the passenger side and headed towards the door. That night we sat out back like we did most nights; me, Joe, and Cameron. I headed off to bed early, and Joe said, "I'm right behind you, bud. Early start for me tomorrow. Roll on Friday." He laughed. I kissed Cameron on the top of the head like I had started to do a lot recently just to say goodnight and headed in.

Cameron woke me the following day and told me she was having lunch with a friend, who I might like, and asked if I would like to join them. I was finding all the girls Cameron was introducing me to were a bit young minded. I'm not saying naïve, but they were sheltered from life. In the UK, I was forced to become an adult at the age of sixteen; here in America, people aren't classed as adults until they turn twenty-one. It's as if they grow up slower than we do, in a more relaxed way of life. I somewhat feel as if I have an advantage over them, as strange as that sounds. I had already learnt to pay bills. I dealt with life's ups and downs in a way that Americans only just started to learn at twenty-one. Joe, who was 28, was closer to my mindset. Dating women Cameron's age was difficult mentally. Don't get me wrong, I did date some of them. It was hard not to. I'm only human. I thanked her and said no thanks as I pulled the cover-up over my head to block out any light.

That night, once we were all back home, we sat in the back, and Joe started talking to Cameron. The first part I got was, "Yeah, I got Thursday and Friday off. I spoke to my father this morning."

"Ok," Cameron said to him in response.

"Do you want to tell him?" Cameron asked Joe.

"No, you go ahead.", He nodded slightly to Cameron.

Cameron said to me, "Hey, Will. Can Joe and I talk to you about something?"

"Yeah, of course," I said and sat forward in my seat. "Everything alright, Cam?" I asked.

Cameron said, "Joe and I sat up last night after you went off to bed talking. We think we might have an idea. I saw how you were yesterday when I got stopped, and you must be on edge every time you see a police car now your visa has expired. What do you think about marrying me?" She smiled. I looked at her, and then I turned towards Joe; I was dumbfounded.

"WHAT?!"

"If we were to get married, you can get a green card and become legal here. You won't have to worry every time the car gets stopped or you see a cop car. I spoke to my parents earlier and explained what your situation was, and they don't mind as long as you sign a prenuptial; my dad just doesn't want you to marry me and take all my inheritance is all," she chuckled. "What do you think?"

"I'm shocked, Cam. How? Sorry, I mean, how can we do this? Are you ok with this?"

Cameron smiled at me and said, "Will, you have done nothing but help me. Well, both of us.' She pointed towards Joe, who smiled at me.

"It's the least we can do to help," Joe replied.

"Joe has booked next Thursday and Friday off so we can jump in the car and go to Las Vegas. We have it all taken care of. You just need to be there and say I do." And she laughed

I sat there, baffled and excited, all in one emotion. "This will make me legal. I will be able to drive," I said out loud, and Joe laughed.

"Great, you can be my cab service for a change." We all laughed together. I knew I had a bond with both Joe and Cameron after Santa Monica, but Cameron being my wife, oh my god, I've made it. Cameron and Joe sat talking about this all evening. I was still in total shock. Joe was winding Cameron up, saying she would be called Cameron Smith and not Reilly anymore.

Cameron laughed and said to me, "Mrs Smith, Will, what do you think, does it suit me?" and smiled toward me.

"You'll make a perfect Mrs Smith Cam," I laughed back as a response.

6

LAND OF OPPORTUNITY

The following Wednesday night, once Joe had finished work, we all jumped in the car and drove five hours over to Las Vegas. We arrived on the Vegas strip just before 11 pm. Joe had booked us into the Bellagio. As we rode up in the elevator toward floor six, where our rooms were, Joe said, "Once we get to our rooms, guys, I'm calling it an early night." Both I and Cameron smiled and nodded towards Joe because we could also feel the day creeping upon us. We left the elevator and headed down the corridor towards our rooms. We all had our own rooms, all three next doors to each other. We suggested that Cameron take the middle room to make her safer with us on either side. We got to our rooms, and all entered simultaneously after wishing each other goodnight.

I was woken early the next morning by Joe. "We have to get moving, bud," he said. "We have a lot to do this morning." Once we had breakfast in the restaurant off the lobby, we went and got a marriage licence from Clark Country City Hall. There were over forty people in line to get the licence.

We got married in a chapel just off the main strip. It was a little awkward when the preacher said to us, "You may kiss the bride." I know on paper now Cameron was my wife, but she's also one of my best friends, who I was starting to see as a little sister. We leaned forward and gazed into her eyes as our lips met. I found myself lingering on the kiss. Her lips seemed so smooth; her tongue delightfully tickled mine. I was really enjoying this. *STOP IT STOP IT.* I pulled backwards. Cameron had her eyes closed. Cam immediately grabbed me and pulled me in again for a hug. Joe let out a "HEYYYYY" with excitement. Joe joined us as we all hugged. We took a few photos, grabbed our stuff, and headed out. We had managed to do all this in one morning. The preacher told us the marriage certificate would arrive in six to eight weeks. We stopped at an all-you-can-eat buffet for lunch, and we ate till until fit to burst. We decided to go back to the hotel for a nap before hitting the casino for our last night. I would like to tell you I enjoyed Las Vegas, but to be completely honest, it was a little too much SHAZAM for my liking.

By the end of ninety-eight, I already had my social security card. I could finally apply for a driving license. I managed to pass after my second attempt. The first time, I was too relaxed; well, that's the excuse I'm telling myself. Cameron had taught me how to drive, mainly as I wouldn't stop asking her until she did. We would drive around in the Stater Bros parking lot once the grocery store was closed, so we had loads of space. Before long, I considered myself a much better driver than Cameron, who had three years on me.

Once I had passed, Cameron and Joe took me to see some guys they knew off Pacific coast highway (PCH) near the pier in Santa Monica. Cam and Joe had arranged for me to test drive a Ford F150. It was white, and the mirrors and bumpers were black. I drove up and down the PCH. This pickup truck had some power. I asked both Joe and Cameron right there how much it was. Neither of them responded to me, but Cameron began negotiations with the dealer. I was over the moon; I could have done cartwheels down the street, not very well, but I would have given it a go. Cameron finished talking and turned to hug me. I hugged her tightly and thanked her. I hugged Joe and thanked him. I felt as if I was a child again. It had been a while since I had become that excited.

In February of ninety-nine, I received a recorded delivery letter at Joe's that had my name emblazoned on it. This was now the second recorded delivery letter I had signed for in my life. It was a brown envelope, and across the front, it had written the "Department of Immigration." I opened the letter as fast as I could. It was my green card. 'It's here', I called out to Joe and Cameron.

Joe got me a job in the construction industry. A close friend of Joe's owned the company. I was building wood-framed houses, anything from three to seven-bedroom properties all over the Los Angeles area. I had taken to the framing and had enjoyed doing carpentry when one night, after a few beers, Joe had talked me into going for my contractor's license. I tried over and over to explain to Joe that my education level isn't that good.

Joe went on to say, "Give it a try. You have nothing to lose." A week later, Joe brought home two books. One was full of mock tests with the answers for the contractor license. The second was a book just on the law. Joe laughed as he slid the books towards me across the table.

"I'll help you, Will. You have just got to memorise the two books from front to back. The law will be easy," Cam said to me. I then remembered Cameron had graduated with honours in business law.

Cameron was true to her word because she always had been and also helped me study. She would read the books repeatedly until I had learned things I never knew my brain could absorb. The contractor's license was harder than the law because the laws themselves are set in stone. Each one just said, you can do this, but no, you can't do that. The contractor's license had me learning pitches of roofers. How low a kitchen ceiling could be, what the minimum opening size of a hatch into the attic had to be, etc. I learnt this stuff over and over again.

In the September of ninety-nine, Cameron came back from

lunch with her friends to tell me she had booked me in with the state license board to take the test. "I'm not ready, Cam," I told her as I was shocked she hadn't said anything before booking me in.

She laughed and said, "You're going to fly through the tests. Trust me, Will you have got this."

In November, I sat for both tests. I was in a room with approximately twenty-five people. We all had a computer screen in front of us. I could feel the butterflies in my stomach. I was on edge as if I had drunk too much coffee that morning. We were all given forty-five minutes to complete each exam. I think the law only took about twenty-five minutes; when I saw a pass mark appear on the screen – 96%. The license itself took me close-up to the time limit. When I clicked send on the computer and sat back in my chair waiting for my answer to appear, I had no idea in my head how I'd done – 92% pass.

"YEAH," I shouted with excitement to see the result come on the screen. I must have been loud because the examiner had asked me to keep it down and that others are still working on their exams. Life was looking good.

In March of 2001, I applied for a position I had seen online in construction. I was happy working for Joe's friend, but his work was sporadic. One month, I would work every day, then he wouldn't have any work for three weeks. This made it difficult to plan anything. The position advertised said you had to have a contractor's licence. The salary caught my eye; the wage was 60-80 thousand a year, depending on experience. The job description was very vague; it only said construction workers with a full license for work in the state of California. The job would require some travelling. That was good with me; travel was my thing. I laughed to myself as I sent in the resume that consisted of mostly jobs me, Joe, and Cameron came up with one night when I told them I need to get a resume together. It was all fabricated. Well, except my last employment, which was Joe's friend and my contractor's license. A few days passed when some young lady called my mobile phone to ask if I'd like to go for an interview.

She explained the job was located all over California that the interviews were to be held in the Hilton hotel in San José. San José wasn't local. It was several hour's drive from me. I accepted the offer of the interview and arranged a Friday morning interview at 11 am. The young lady gave me the address, wished me a good day, and hung up.

On the morning of the interview, I was up and showered early. Joe had lent me the BMW to make a good first impression. Both he and Cameron laughed as they had discussed the chances of my pickup being able to make the journey there and back. I left just before five am, set the GPS, sat nav up, and drove the five-plus hours north to San José.

I watched as the sun rose in the distance behind a vista of mountains. I arrived at the Hilton hotel quicker than I had anticipated. I have 40 minutes, which gave me just enough time to change my shirt, have a few cigarettes, and get myself composed and ready after the long journey. I kept thinking to myself; I wish I had a Starbucks Mocha Frappuccino right now. It was hot in San José but not as hot as the southern part of California. However, it was still a lot warmer than Liverpool. I lit a cigarette up.

It had been nearly three years since I first arrived here. How my life has already changed in ways, I could never have imagined or expected. I laughed as I thought back to my days of first going into Redbank and the lads I had met along the way. Before I knew it, the time had gone. I did a quick change of shirts outside the car, sprayed myself with deodorant, which was a trick I learnt from Joe. I always kept a deodorant can close by to freshen myself up when needed. I knew Joe kept a spray in his glovebox as I'd used it so many times before. I shut the BMW door and locked it, had two more pulls on my cigarette, then dropped it to the floor and stood on it. "I'm ready," I said confidently in my mind and headed towards the main entrance.

As I walked across the parking lot, I could feel a breeze in the air. This was like an English summer's day. Not that England got that many sunny days. As I'm nearing the entrance, the valet man, all dressed smartly in his burgundy Hilton uniform, greeted me with a "Good morning sir" and a smile on his face.

I greeted him back politely. I thanked him as he held the door open for me as I walked through. As soon as I cleared the doorway, I could feel the crisp, cool air coming from the AC. I looked around quickly as I walked further into the lobby. On either side of the pathway, directly in front of me, were seating areas, with what looked like very comfy black leather seats and a lobby desk right behind. Even the floor was covered in large, shiny black tiles. There was the occasional rug placed around the floor. I continue my walk towards the desk. I can see a youngish-looking lady in her early twenties; she has dark brown hair styled in a bob cut. She was also wearing a burgundy Hilton uniform.

"Good morning, sir," she said in a very clear voice as she looked up from a book she was reading.

I responded with, "Good morning, I'm here for an interview with a gentleman called Bernard Schmitts", and showed her the spelling on the piece of paper I had written during the interview call. I smiled towards her. The receptionist smiled back.

"If you go right here and pass the two elevators, the first door you come to is the room you're after; it's on the left side of the corridor." I thanked her and headed in the direction she had explained to me. I passed the two elevators and was nearing the door. As I grew closer to the door, I could see it was ajar. I tapped firmly on the door, which opened it in the process.

I heard a male voice shout, "come in", upon which I entered. I quickly absorb my surroundings. The room was bright and warm from the sun entering the large windows.There was a very large dark wooden table, which took up three-quarters of the room and had eight chairs surrounding it. Sitting right at the head of the table was a gentleman. He began to rise as I entered the room. As I neared towards him, passing the chairs on the side of the table, I raised my hand in anticipation of his hand greeting mine.

"Good morning," I said, as he had fully risen now and was shaking my hand firmly.

He responded quite sharply. "Good morning, Bernard Schmitts. Are you William?" in what appeared to sound like a German or possibly an Austrian accent. He released my hand from the shake and gestured for me to have a seat.

I responded, "Yes, Will. Was that Schmit you said? "I paused quickly. "Do I detect a European accent?" in an inquisitive tone. I sat down in the seat that was already pulled out from what I think was the last interviewer.

"No, it's Schmitts," and with a small pause and a little adjustment in his seat as he sat back down, "please just call me Bernard," with a smile. He jumped straight back in with, "the accent is German." I had been to Germany with my backpacking travels some years earlier.

"Oh, which part?"

He said the name, but it was a place I never heard of or been to. We talked about Europe, and I told him about my work in Germany; needless to say, I didn't tell him the whole truth, but only what sounded fun and exciting. I could see he enjoyed reminiscing about his home country. This somewhat lightened the interview and made it more relaxing. He went on to tell me all about the position he was offering. He started to explain what he was looking for, and for the next ten minutes, I sat and listened.

The position was updating all the ATM teller machines for Lincoln Cargo banks. I would be loading up the New ATM and surrounds at the warehouse. Then I would drive the new ATM to the bank, meeting two Wincapa Bixdorf employers on-site – a computer technician and helper. Wincapa was the biggest supplier of ATMs in Germany, if not Europe. The work would be 3-6 days per week, Sunday to Friday. Depending on how many ATMs Wincapa Bixdorf could schedule with the banks themselves. We would be removing the old ATM for the new ATM, changing the plastic surrounding on the outside of the building or ATM location.

The new ATMs we would be installing were what was called paperless, with no receipts printed, only on-screen balances. They no longer need to fill out a form or find an envelope to put the money in. Now they are becoming a lot easier to function and more climate friendly. It sounded easy. I sat back in my seat to continue listening once the ATM and surroundings were finished. To have "GONE LIVE" was the term Bernard used to make sure the ATM worked for customers to use. This must be done between the hours of 9 am and 5.30 pm, or the banking hours. If the ATM isn't live, then Wincapa Bixdorf must pay a $5000 penalty fine. Once this is all done, and we have the thumbs up from the bank manager or supervisor, I would load up the truck and take everything back to the warehouse to be recycled.

Initially, the position would be local to the Los Angeles area, but after three months, it would involve loading the truck on Sunday for the week with three to five ATMs and new surrounds and staying in hotels each night. With a new job and location each day. On the Friday, I would drive the truck back to the warehouse, unload, and go home. He explained how I would be given a company credit card to purchase any tools or equipment required, pay for fuel for the truck, and all my meals. This alone sounded like an amazing deal, but the salary was anywhere from $60 – 80 thousand a year. He explained that if I was offered the position, I would be trained for the first two weeks by a set of different contractors like myself, so I wasn't just being thrown in at the deep end. I would be paid for the training if the position was offered to me. After he finished explaining things to me, he asked me what starting salary I would accept if the position was offered to me? I responded quickly with a very confident tone. "I would expect the full 80, this position is going to take up all my time, which I'm okay with, but I will be giving up so much." He smiled towards me as if he fully appreciated that I was straightforward with him. Maybe it was a European thing, but I'm sure that hadn't been the answer most interviewers would have said. As Bernard showed me back to the lobby and thanked me for attending, I knew I would be offered the position in my gut.

I was super excited about telling Joe and Cameron all about

my interview later that evening. Joe asked me if I was okay working away all the time. I told him hell yeah, I would be okay with that.

"I will be meeting people, making great money, and I can still party at the weekend."

Cameron laughed and said, "You'd better come home on the weekends."

"Of course I will, Cam. Are you going to miss me?" as I grinned like a Cheshire cat towards her.

The following day, the position was mine. Bernard had also agreed to the 80 I requested. For the next few weeks, I settled into the job. I knew by the third day I was going to love this job, being outside in the sun all day. Don't get me wrong, the job wasn't easy by far, but once the ATM was off the back of the truck, it got easier. Bernard had thought of everything. He rented a huge 24 ft truck. It had taken me a while to drive this confidently, as it was a monster. Bernard made sure that it came with a tail lift to get the ATMs in and out of the truck, so using a pallet and pallet jack, the ATM moved with no problem. I bought every tool I figured I might need. I put it all on the company credit card. I bought things on the off chance I might need them in the future. I was really starting to enjoy this job, a new place every day, sun shining and being paid an amazing salary.

After about roughly three months into the job, I would load the truck on a Sunday and leave for wherever Bernard had assigned me. I would check into a hotel that Wincapa pre-arranged to ensure there was safe parking for the truck. The ATMs were all empty, but that wouldn't stop anyone from stealing all the tools. I got to work in the day, then back to the hotel, park up, have some food, and sleep. The next day was exactly the same. I didn't mind. In fact, I was really enjoying it. I was constantly meeting new people. It's incredible how many people stop to talk to me once they heard the accent. I met a few females along the way; however, I wouldn't say I'm a sailor with a woman in every port.

The first place I went to was the Redlands, off the 10 freeway in San Bernardino. The drive only took an hour; it was roughly about fifty miles away from the Los Angeles area. Redlands wasn't a massive city like LA, but it was still a big town. Lincoln cargo had three different banks in the city limits. All three banks had two ATMs. So at one ATM per day, I spent two weeks in the Redland. I found a fantastic Italian restaurant just two minutes walk away from my hotel, and there was a bar right next door so I could have a nightcap. From there, I never looked back, working the perfect job in the perfect weather. Was this the perfect life?

7

DREW & CHRISTOPHER

I had moved around quite a lot since the Redlands area. I have seen more Californian back towns then 'Billy the kid'. From my driving, it t was looking like all the banks so far we're off the ten freeways, give or take anyway. I had a four-day week in Yucaipa. This place was hot and right at the very end of San Bernardino County, surrounded by mountains and desert land. The temperature on Tuesday had been 110 degrees, which was accepted as a normal day here. The town had two banks or four ATMs. On the Thursday, the last day of the week, when the workday was over, I looked forward to a few cold ones and some food that evening. I went back to the hotel to clean up before heading out.

I stepped into the hotel lobby on my way out to search for a bar. I spoke to the young man behind the reception desk. I asked him if he knew of any local bars within walking distance. He recommended a bar that was around a five minutes walk away called the 'Top Dog Tavern.' He smiled at me as he told me the women who go there hardly wore any clothes. I laughed and thought, well, why not. I thanked him and set about in the direction he had explained to me.

I needed a couple of beers in a bar, a little food, and an early night before heading back to the warehouse first thing to unload. After this, the rest of Friday would be my own to enjoy. Well, that was my plan or thoughts for the evening, anyways. I had arranged to go to a new nightclub with Cameron and Joe on Saturday evening. It was supposed to be the biggest nightclub in the Los Angeles area, and we had been placed on the VIP list because the girls knew the owner. We had only heard about STARZ the night club from friends of Cameron's

I headed straight towards the bar. Turning a corner, it came into view situated at the end of a row of businesses in front of me. The place was smaller than I had imagined, but to be fair, I had no idea. Just like the previous towns I'd visited with work, I was constantly going in blind, as they say.

As I entered through the doors, I noticed the staff at the door: two young ladies wearing white tank tops and denim shorts. "Good evening," one of them said, "you can sit anywhere you like." I thanked her and walked towards the table in the corner to take a seat. The bar smelled clean, which was unique. A woman roughly aged 27 was heading towards me smiling; she also wore a white tank top and denim shorts. I could see the lace of her bra sticking out of the tank top. She had long brown hair, to which she had tied back, and her eyes were hazel in colour. The shape of her body was, well, let's just say yes, please, and leave it at that.

"Can I get you a drink, babe?" she said as she stopped in front of my table.

"Yes, please. Coors Light, if you don't mind," I responded with a smile. Then we did the usual two-minute small talk thing, that by now I've come to expect when I speak and people hear my accent,

"Are you English?"

"Yeah," I respond. They usually have a family member living, visiting, or they have been themselves to England or some story to tell me about the UK. After a few minutes, I got my Coors and sat back to enjoy the evening. I had done this in most of the towns, mostly as staying in a different hotel every couple of days becomes boring fast.

After about my third beer, a lady approached me. I had seen her for the past hour, at the front of the bar playing on the fruit machine and talking to the hostesses. As she became closer, she smiled and asked me, "want to play a game of pool?"

"Sure, why not" I responded. The lady was roughly around 27 years old, had dark brown straight hair, a little longer than shoulder-length, and her eyes were brown. She's wearing a pair of pink shorts and a shoulderless black top. I introduced myself, and she told me her name was Drew. We played a few games of pool. I played very badly; pool was never my thing. We filled the jukebox with loose change, selecting the music we both liked and sat together, talking and drinking all evening. I enjoyed Drew's company and, as an added improvement, she wasn't too bad looking either. I just knew we wouldn't work as a couple, though, because of our different paths in life. By 9 pm, I told Drew I had to leave and call it a night. I had to be up early the next morning to head back to the warehouse.

As I was leaving, Drew passed me a small piece of paper, "my phone number', she said. "Just in case, you're ever in the area again," and she reached in to kiss me on the cheek. I said my goodbyes to the bartender on my way out and headed back towards the hotel.

As I had walked this way a little earlier, I spotted a little restaurant just across the road from me. I figured I'd go there to grab some food because it was so close to the hotel. As I neared the place and was attempting to cross the road, I looked and saw the name CASA CAMINO in large letters across the face of the building. I crossed the road and approached the door to enter. On the window, there was a sign saying family-owned restaurant. I had some soft-shelled tacos for dinner, followed by steak with cheese. The place was a little run down, but the tacos were exceptional. After I finished and paid at the desk, I left and headed back towards the hotel. I had run across the road to get back to the side my hotel was on and suddenly heard my name being called. I turned my head to see who had called me. It was Drew; she was coming up behind me. "Hey, where are you going?" I asked her as she became nearer.

"I'm heading home, Will," she said, and before I had a chance to acknowledge it, she added, "Would you like to come back for a drink or something?"

"The 'or something' sounds interesting." I chuckled.

"Come on," she said as she wrapped her arms around mine to guide me and started laughing. We got back to her place, and she got me a drink. She put some music on, and we began talking. After about 5 minutes, I could see Drew was looking at my lips as I spoke. *Are we about to kiss?* Suddenly Drew pushed forward towards me and started kissing me. I could feel her fingers combing through the back of my head. I pulled her in closer towards me. Drew immediately started pulling my belt open, then my trousers. I could feel it as she grabbed my hand and placed it on her breast. I pushed forward with my mouth to continue kissing. Then suddenly, Drew jumped back on the couch as if to put some distance between us. It was then I heard a key turning in the lock on the front door.

I looked at Drew, and her face changed in less than a split second from smiling to worry. The front door opened, and some guy walked in. He didn't fill the doorway as he entered and could only have been five foot six, maybe seven at the very most. He had longish hair that he had combed backwards and was clean-shaven. I judged him to be roughly about my age. As soon as our eyes met, he immediately set towards me, "WHO ARE YOU?" he shouted towards me as I looked back at him, all confused. I looked towards Drew and then back at him. Drew was sat frozen on the couch. She looked terrified. The guy was on top of me now and started throwing punches towards me. I did all I could to stop him, but he was relentless.

I shouted back to him, "WHAT'S GOING ON? STOP!" He didn't and continued trying to make a punch connect while screaming. I pushed him back to get him off me and realised he was only light. I shoved him hard, and he went backwards. I launched to my feet. "HANG ON," I shouted, but this didn't stop him; he came towards me again. By this time, I had reached my feet and stood upright. I punched back as he neared me again. With my first punch, I hit him square in the face, and he looked dazed. I then hit him again, and he fell backwards to the floor but immediately started to get back up again.

Drew has now jumped off the couch and was moving towards me. She is screaming at me, "leave him alone, leave him alone." As soon as she's close enough, she starts punching me in the side of the head. I cover up the best I can, and the man is now on all fours getting back up. I push Drew back, but she runs right back towards me.

"That's enough, I screamed and swung my fist out towards her. I had thrown the punch randomly to stop anyone else from hitting me. When I punched her, I knew she was out, as her body dropped straight to the floor. This was my first time hitting a woman. I had never even so much as argued with previous sexual partners. The guy was up and was coming towards me. He managed to get his hands around my throat even as I was throwing every punch I had in me. Finally, I had connected and could feel it. He went down and stayed down. He fell over face forward straight into the arm of the couch and bounced off to the side onto the floor. My heart was pounding in my chest. "What the fuck?" I said out loud. Neither of them moved or stirred. I walked towards Drew, who had landed at the side of the couch. As I got closer and kneeled beside her, I heard him moving and grunting slightly. I jumped to my feet and went straight towards him. I punched him as he lay on the floor. Once, then twice, and the second punch made his body go limp again. The next few seconds could have been hours with thoughts racing around my mind like rats in a maze.

Oh my god!

Should I run?

They might call the police.

Should I call the police and tell them what happened? I thought about what Cameron had said to me in Santa Monica that they would blame me. I am, after all, in her place. *Who the fuck is he? What the fuck was he thinking?*

I would like to say the thought of running out of the room was the first thing on my mind, but it wasn't. I knew what I had to do. My heart rate began climbing rapidly.I wasn't panicking or worried at this point; my mind had already decided what my body was going to do. I pulled my belt off my jeans that Drew had just loosened minutes earlier. I wrapped it around his neck and started pulling. As I pulled tighter on the belt, his whole body began to jerk. He woke and began to struggle and squirm with all his might. He had no chance. I had a hold of the belt and wasn't letting go. He was mine now. He held on for a short time and urinated just before he gave up his fight. His body fell limp and no longer resisted. I held the belt for a little longer, pulling it tighter again with my hands. I was hurting my own hands as the belt cut into my palms. As I released the grip I had on the belt, the weight of his body slumped to the floor. I pulled the belt free of his neck.

I stood up and went straight towards Drew "your next" I muttered under my breath, as she was still lying unconscious at the side of the couch. I wrapped the belt around her neck and started pulling from behind. Within a couple of seconds, she woke up and tried to struggle, but it was too late. As I pulled even harder on the belt, I said "just give in". Drew had more fight in her than the guy. She struggled, kicking her legs wildly and, in the process, pushed the couch back a few inches into the wall behind.

Eventually, she stopped resisting and was gone. I took the belt off, sat down on the edge of the couch, and looked at what I had just done. I would like to say I was scared or had some fear of being caught, but I didn't. My heart was beating repeatedly. My only thought was how I can remove as much evidence of myself from this room as possible. I couldn't bury these two like Daryl and Robert. How was I going to move them? It's not like I can just bury them in the back garden. I paced around the room, thinking. If it was one thing my mind was good at, it was solving problems. I had put myself in enough positions over the years to learn a lot of escape routes. I decided they had to stay. I couldn't get the two bodies out of this house, even if I had the truck in the front. It's a residential neighbourhood, and someone will see me. Even if I could get them out, how was I going to find a place? And, dig a hole, and get back to the warehouse as if nothing was wrong by lunchtime? I found myself laughing hysterically, and the adrenaline was flowing through my body as fast as my blood could carry it.

My brain set about solving the problem, and my body followed suit. I went about my clean up as thoroughly as I had with Daryl and Robert. I went into the kitchen and found some scissors and black bags. I wiped any surface or handle I had touched with the tea towel draped over the oven handle. I walked calmly back into the front room. Drew was the smallest of the two, so I started with her. I cut Drew's clothes off first and bagged each item. When I removed the pink shorts she had on, just below her panty line, I noticed she had a blue butterfly tattoo sitting on top of a small red rose on her navel. Once she was completely naked, I dragged her by her wrists into the bathroom and pushed her body into the bathtub turning on the cold faucet.

I headed back to the room and started on the guy who lay motionless. I cut his shirt off first; he had an American flag tattoo on his chest and two initials tattooed on his left forearm: TL and a little red heart. The heart had faded over the years, and the letters had started to spread out, which made them harder to make out. *Maybe his child or an ex-partner*? As I cut his jeans off, I pulled his wallet out of his pocket and flicked it open. I recalled doing the same thing with Daryl and Robert previously. As if I was reliving the moment, the identification wasn't the same as mine or Californian. It was from the state of Missouri. The driving licence said Christopher Lambert, 31 years old, and the address on it was in Branson, Missouri. I had no idea where Missouri was, never mind Branson. There was no money in the wallet; it was just full of receipts from stores for all sorts of items. I put the wallet in the bag and removed the rest of Christopher's clothing.

I left him lying on the floor as I rushed back to the bathroom quickly to check the water level. It was not even a quarter of the way full yet; I turned the faucet off. I went back to the front room, composed myself, and then dragged Christopher's body into the bathroom.

Christopher was a little harder to get into the bathtub. Once I got him on the rim of the bathtub, he dropped right on top of Drew's body. I grabbed the towel off the back of the door and started the faucet back up. Using the shampoo on the side of the tub, I set about cleaning both of their bodies from head to toe. As they lay in the tub to make sure every bit of evidence was erased. I scrubbed the inside of Drew's mouth because we had kissed, and traces of my saliva would still be in her mouth. When I was sure both bodies were clean, I turned the faucet off and pulled the plug from the water. I took the showerhead down off the wall and turned the faucet back on. I clicked the showerhead on and began to rinse their bodies off until all the soap suds had disappeared down the plughole. I put the plug back in and turned the hot tap on fully. As the bathtub was filling, I walked back into the front room and started using the towel to clean up anywhere I might have possibly touched. At the side of the couch, I came across a black leather women's bag. I looked in and saw a small black purse. I reached in and pulled the purse out, flipping it open. The identification was also from Missouri: Drew Lambert. My first thought was brother and sister; somehow, my brain thinks differently. It was only a split second before I said out loud and startled myself in the silence. "THEY'RE MARRIED".

Before I turned the faucet off, I waited until the bathtub was filled to the very top with hot water. The steam in the bathroom alone was making me light-headed. I grabbed the shampoo bottle I had used on the side of the bathtub and stood up. Leaving the door open, I left the room and put the nearly empty shampoo bottle in the black bag. I had a full black bag to take with me. It was less than a five-minute walk back to the truck and the hotel. If I don't get seen from here to there, I'll be ok. I opened the front door with the towel, then placed the towel in the black bag. I picked up my bottle of Budweiser and drank what was left, dropping the empty bottle into the bag. I tied the black bag up. I grabbed the bag in one hand and used my foot to pull the front door shut behind me.

I could hear cars in the distance, but nothing on this street. I went for it; I wasn't running; in fact, I wasn't walking too fast either. I was just careful. I walked back to the hotel as if I was a ghost; I didn't see a single soul or a moving car until I got back to the road my hotel was on. Only then did I see a car turning around at the end of the street. I reached in my pocket, pulled the keys out for the truck, and quietly put the bag of clothes in the truck. I will deal with that once I'm out of Yucaipa. I went up to my room and sat on the end of the bed, smoking a cigarette. Time had flown by as my mind was replaying the whole night's events. I was seen in the bar with Drew, but I left an hour before her to eat. Surely no one will have seen me when I left the restaurant. I ended up laughing loudly to myself as I thought about all the scenarios of what-ifs. I rubbed my hands across my face. I got undressed and put my clothes in a plastic bag. I jumped in the shower to clean myself. Once I had finished and stepped out to dry, I lit up my last cigarette for the day and sat on the toilet to smoke it. "Sleep, you need sleep," I said to myself out loud. I dropped the half-smoked cigarette in the toilet and stood up. I exited the doorway, and as I passed the light switch, I flicked the light off and climbed into bed. I could faintly hear the room next door talking as I slipped off to sleep.

8

CHRISTOPHER COLUMBUS

I woke up early the next morning. Peeking under the blinds, the sun had disturbed me and forced me to get up. I recalled the previous evening. Why wasn't I worried about being caught last night? I lay there staring at the hotel ceiling. I'm not heartless, right? I couldn't lay here all morning just thinking. I knew I had to get moving. I jumped in the shower quickly, packed my suitcase, and checked out of the hotel. I was heading down the 10 freeway. I knew I had the bag of clothes and identifications to dispose of, but that would have to wait. I've got to get back to the warehouse. I finally pulled into the warehouse at 1.30 pm. I did the usual meet and greet with the warehouse staff and set about unloading. By 2.15 pm, I was finished, the truck was cleaned out, and I headed home.

When I got home, there was a note on the patio doors from Cameron. "Gone for lunch with Jess", with a blotched kiss from Cameron kissing the paper with her lipstick on. I grabbed a Coors and sat at the table on the patio. The sun was hot on my face. I pulled my shirt off and slipped into my seat. My head began processing everything that had happened.

. . .

I ended up in some bad places. I realised I have the blood of four people on my hands. My mind started to wonder; I had no control over it; I just sat there and allowed it to show me the thought patterns one step at a time slowly. I am a murderer. I could have stopped after I knocked him down, but I didn't. I became enraged. I lost control. My body was acting, and my mind was willing it on. I had never had this before; I had a few fights in my life. Some I lost, and some I won, but I never to this extent. What have I done? This thought echoed inside my mind? Am I evil? Will I be going to hell now? Not that I fully believe in religion anyway. It was strange; I somewhat enjoyed my mind raced back and forth with emotions. Why did I automatically start cleaning up? I saw the two dead bodies as a cleanup. Do I have no respect for people any longer? Of course, you do; I heard my brain fighting. You love Joe and Cameron. I remembered reading a book on how some killers enjoy watching their victims die. Did I enjoy killing? I could feel myself becoming excited.

My mind began thinking of serial killers. Am I a serial killer? It flashed through my mind. NO, NO, I'm not sick or twisted in the head. I'm nothing like "Jack the Ripper", the first name that sprung to my mind. I am a serial killer now though, because the authorities classify anyone who murders three or more people to be serial killers. I recalled reading in a magazine article that psychologists suspect in every state in America there were at least two to three serial killers operating simultaneously. No, I can't be, surely? We all know serial killers; some are so famous we know them more than we know the royal family. There was a conspiracy that a royal family member could have been "Jack the Ripper."

I'm not like that. I'm not sick in the head. I don't cut bodies up. I don't kill for gain, or profit, or even sexual gratification. I'm not perverted. My brain was going over and over everything in my life in a mere flash of time. I sat thinking until I heard Cameron's voice shouting my name. She came out smiling as she saw me.

"How was work, babe?" she said and before I had finished

saying "same old thing", she screamed, "STARZ tonight." It was then I realised we had the nightclub to go to tonight.

"Oh yeah, I forgot," as I chuckled to myself. With all that had happened in the last twenty-four hours, it had completely slipped my mind. We sat around just chatting. Cameron was hoping to bump into Roland, the guy she liked, who she had introduced me to in another nightclub. We sat drinking a few more beers until Joe came home. As soon as I heard his car in the garage, I grabbed him a beer and handed it to him as he walked through the door. I walked back out to the patio and put the remaining beers on the table. I pulled a seat from the table out for Joe. I passed Cameron another bottle and sat back in my seat.

Joe came straight out the back and shouted towards Cameron and me, "let the weekend begin," and then started dancing. Both Cameron and I cheered him on, whistling. Joe attempted to do the robot, which had us both crying with laughter. This was just what I needed to relax after everything that had transpired. We had some pizza delivered for dinner and got ready to go out.

All three of us squeezed into the back seat of the taxicab for the ride into Los Angeles. We arrived at STARZ just after eleven and had our table in the VIP lounge. Cameron's friends Jess and Kristen showed up. It was all thanks to Jess that we had the table. Jess had slept with the owner a few weeks back, and he had become besotted with her. He would constantly be texting or calling her. It made me wonder how good Jess would be between the sheets. My mind somewhat drifted off to thinking about both Jess and Kristen between the sheets together. Kristen grabbed Joe's arm, and Cameron grabbed mine as we headed to the dance floor. We saw a lot of people we had met in previous clubs. I saw Tameka, and we kissed gently and asked how each other was doing. Meka had a guy stood right behind her. She gave me the eyes to ask me to say nothing in front of him about her and me. I wouldn't have said anything either way. I knew what I had with Meka was purely sexual. We bumped into Roland again after Cameron dragged us across the dance floor to put us in talking distance. I didn't speak to him myself, just waved towards him. I was too busy taking in the nightclub and all the people that were dancing around me.

Roland and his friend had seen Cameron and started dancing with them, so we all danced together. I caught myself watching Jess and Kristen dancing. My eyes looked at all 3 of them, and my heart rate started climbing. I was sexually attracted to both. Cameron had warned me off prior as it wasn't a good idea. I suddenly found my stare had moved towards Cameron. I was watching her hips move as she swayed to the music. I could see the outline of the thong she was wearing. For a small moment, I imagined myself pulling the thong slowly down. Cameron turned around in her dance and made eye contact with me. She smiled at me and then at Joe. She danced towards me.

Cam leaned in towards me, she whispered in my ear. "I just saw you checking my ass out." She immediately smiled and turned back towards Jess and Kristen, and continued dancing. *Oh my God* raced through my head. Cameron has just caught me checking out her ass. *What the fuck,* Will. Stop that; she's one of your best friends. The night flew by, but it always did when we all got together.

Just before 2.30 am, we all left the nightclub. Joe had met some girl just after midnight that Cameron had introduced him to. He spent most of the evening chatting and giggling with her. I just had a great night with Cameron, Jess, and Kristen. Although it was mostly Jess and Kristen, Cameron spent the night pushing up on Roland, who she seemed to be getting on with really well. He even hugged her as a slow song came on at the end of the evening. The two of them swayed back and forth, dancing in each other's arms. We said our goodbyes to the people we had met in the club and decided to head home.

After we left the club, the sea breeze was cold at first, and it took some time for my body to adjust. A slight wind made me feel cold after moving around for so long on a hot dance floor. As we walked along Meadow drive approaching Hollywood Blvd, Jess rushed into the bushes and started throwing up. We had all been drinking a lot tonight, but Jess had started drinking well before she went out. Joe grabbed me by the arm and pulled me to one side as both Kristen and Cameron began helping Jess. "Hey bud," he said quietly. "Can I leave the ladies with you? You arrange to get everyone home. This date of mine wants to go at it yesterday."

I laughed and told him, "GO, GO, I got this, get going. I'll see you at home." Joe and his date said goodbye very quickly and set off. As Joe walked away, I smiled. I was happy for Joe because it had been a while since he had any female company. He deserved this. I chuckled to myself, imagining Joe on top of his date.

"I'M OK, IM OK," Jess shouted as she began to walk in front of us down towards the taxicab rank. Cameron and Kristen both looked at me and laughed. We let Jess and Kristen take the first cab and got the one right after. Once we got home, Cameron and I grabbed a few beers, got our swimming costumes, and sat in the hot hub. The water's temperature was a little hot at first in the cool night, but once we settled in, we began enjoying it. We watched as the sun came up in the distance behind the city of Los Angeles. By about 6.30 in the morning, I was ready for sleep. Cameron agreed; we got out and started drying. Cameron cleaned up the table quickly, binning the empty beer bottles we had littered around the hot tub. I kissed Cameron on the forehead and said goodnight. I went into my room, took off my wet shorts, and dropped them into the shower. I closed the bedroom curtains as the early morning sunlight was beginning to heat the room and climbed into bed.

I began to drift away with the thoughts of the killer Ted Bundy and the way he had killed for sex. I was nothing like him. I didn't kill for sex. What type of serial killer am I going to be classified as? I was suddenly shocked for a split second picturing myself being caught. I had a picture in my head of being surrounded by armed cops. This thought was disturbed by a light tapping on the bedroom door. The door opened, and the pitch-dark room was now lit up from the hallway light. It was Cameron. She stepped into the room and closed the door, and she said, "Are you still awake, Will? Can I talk to you about something?"

"I'm naked, Cam. I'm not even under the covers."

Cameron laughed at me and said, "oh yeah, about that." I could just make out her shape as she moved onto the bed beside me. She moved straight towards me, and before I had time to react, she had started kissing me. I grabbed her and pulled her into me, and started kissing her back. I wasn't the only one naked. I could feel the skin of her breasts rub on my chest. As my hand slid down her neck, I cupped her breasts and started caressing her nipples.

"STOP WILL," my mind shouted at me. I wasn't stopping; my body loved the feeling of her soft skin on my body. I could feel myself waking up. "I want to taste you." I pulled Cameron towards me, laying her on her back, as I sat on the edge of the bed. I pushed her legs open with force as if to say, and now you're mine. Cameron gave a gentle gasp as my head was aimed towards her midsection. I took Cameron in my mouth, and as I did, she pushed back. I started sucking gently.

"Don't stop, Will," Cameron gasped as her whole back arched up from the bed.

It was then the reality slapped me in the face. "NO, NO, WE CAN'T DO THIS, CAM." I pushed away from Cameron sharply. I distanced myself from the bed. "I'm sorry, Cam. I can't; you're my best friend. If we sleep together, it will destroy everything. I can't let that happen. I'm sorry, Cameron," I said. Cameron moved towards me again on the bed.

"But Will, I saw you looking at me earlier. I know you have feelings towards me. When we got married, the kiss you gave me in the chapel in Vegas had feelings in it. I could feel your passion, Will. I want you to. I have wanted you since the first day we met," she said. I also wanted her, but I didn't say that. I wanted so much to taste her again to have her in my mouth. To enjoy her.

"I'm sorry, Cam, that was only a friendly kiss. I was making it look real for the photos."

"I know that wasn't just a friendly kiss, but something more than that, Will," she said.

I managed to convince Cam that it was with some time. I could taste Cameron in my mouth still. Before long, it was like the last hour hadn't even happened. We laughed it off to drinking and blamed Jess for the tequila shots. We moved past the awkward moment where we nearly did. Maybe, it's because we were drunk and laughed at each other. Before long, we had both curled up on the bed. Cameron had her head on my chest, and her leg bent over mine. I could smell the sweetness of Cameron's body. Was I right to stop? Should I have stopped? Would I stop after sex or lost it? Would she end up like Drew and her husband? I couldn't hurt Cameron. I love her. What kind of love rushed around my thoughts? I couldn't stop thinking about how sweet she tasted and soon fell asleep with a grin on my face.

I woke the next morning to find Cameron had already left the room. My body just lay there as my thoughts began jumping around inside my head. You nearly fucked Cameron last night.

Indecision plagued my thoughts. I thought back to when I strangled Drew and her husband. The adrenaline rush was incredible. I wonder why he pissed himself when I strangled him? She hadn't. I was only there to sleep with Drew. How the hell was I supposed to know she was married? I had enjoyed it. I found myself smiling from ear to ear as I lay there. I want to do it again. I want to plan it next time. The people who have died so far had just been events that I had no control over. THE NEXT TIME WILL BE MY WAY.

I lost my train of thought as I heard Cameron exit her bedroom and walk past my bedroom door. I wondered to myself how awkward it would be to see Cameron this morning. I nearly didn't stop. We fell asleep naked in each other's arms; I wondered what she must have thought when she initially woke up on top of my naked body. I got up, showered, and put my shorts on. Just to check, he was fine, I called Joe even though he didn't answer. I got a text message from him minutes later.

I'm good, bud, speak later, ☺

I left my room and walked towards the kitchen. I could smell the coffee. I walked into the kitchen, and Cameron was just pouring me a cup.

"Good morning sexy, we drank lots last night. How the hell did we get home?" she said. Did she not remember the events of last night? Should I say something? I didn't.

I smiled at her and kissed her on the forehead, saying, "Good morning, Hun." However, it dawned on me it was very nearly lunchtime. "We got a taxi; we were all wasted. I bet Jess has a hangover this morning," I laughed.

"She was out of it, wasn't she," laughed Cameron. I think we all were out of it a little bit and laughed as we took our coffees to the patio. It was a little overcast today, still very sunny but cloudy. The warm breeze was quite relaxing since it was usually hot air. I caught the scent of Cameron's hair as she walked in front of me towards the patio table. I looked at her and thought how only a few hours earlier I wanted her. I found I had stopped still in my tracks and watched as she pulled the umbrella up on the table. After we had a couple of cups of coffee each, Cameron said out the middle of nowhere, "I woke up naked in bed with you this morning," as she looked me right in the face.

"Did you?" I said in a confused tone. "We must have passed out together." We chuckled to each other, so she had forgotten or was she just trying to see what I remembered? "What do you recall about last night, Cam," I asked her so I could find out what she remembered. She told me how right up to the taxi ride home that she was fine; she couldn't recall after that. I told her that we just had a few drinks in the hot tub and then went to bed, she must have climbed in with me during the night, and maybe she woke up cold. We laughed it off. She told me how loud my snoring was as I slept and how this had woke her up.

We sat outside like we did most weekends until Joe came home in the early evening and told us all about his conquest in the early hours of the morning. He told us how Beverly, the woman he had left with, liked to be choked during sex. This had freaked Joe out, and it wasn't his thing. I had never tried it, well, not during sex anyway. Not even with Meka, and we experimented with a lot of kinky things. We talked about what we would like to do next weekend and the week we had coming up. I let them know I'd be gone by the time they surface on Sunday. I knew both would sleep in. I said my goodnights and headed to bed. Back on the road again tomorrow, a new town, a new chapter in my life.

9

MADISON RECUPIDO AND CHASE BAKER

Beaumont, California, and Banning were my next two destinations. There were three banks with a total of eight ATMs between them to swap over, which would take around two weeks. The hotel was two minutes off the freeway exit. On the first day, the ATMs were already live, and so my day was over by 3.30 pm. I dropped my bag off at the hotel room and set out to find myself a cold beer. I turned the corner on my hotel street to see a Mexican restaurant right next door. "Juan Pollas," I said out loud while walking through the door. I entered the small, dark lobby area with a pair of glass doors on my left and my right. I looked in the door on the right, then the door on the left. The door to the right went into the restaurant, and the door to the left went into the bar. I would grab a cold one first, I thought, pulling open the left glass door and walking inside. The bar wasn't very big, roughly about ten ft long and was relatively bright compared to the lobby. In front of the bar was a line of bar stools, and behind them sat tables and chairs. There was another door at the end of the bar with a sign saying pool above it. I walked halfway down the bar only to see a woman a few years younger than me, maybe twenty-seven, with blonde wavy hair and blue eyes staring at me.

"What can I get you, babe?" she asked as I pulled a bar stool out and sat down next to her.

"Coors Light, please," rolled off my tongue with ease as I smiled towards her. She walked off to get our drinks, and as she did, I managed to seize the chance to get a good look at her. She wore skin-tight jeans, a pair of white converse baseball boots, and a seriously out of shape white t-shirt. It wasn't wholly see-through; however, it was easy to make out the lacy pattern of the pinkish bra she had on beneath. She couldn't have been more than five foot five, although it was hard to judge because she stood on a raised step behind the bar. She gave me my drink, and we stood and talked until the next customer came in and sat at the end of the bar by the door. The bartender, a local girl who had never been out of the state before, named Chase, was very interesting to talk to, but I also imagined she was great between the sheets. The bar got steadily busy as the night went on, and so, in the meantime, I went next door and had some food. Afterwards, I returned to the bar for a quick nightcap. Chase grabbed me a Coors as soon as she saw me coming back in.

The bar was a lot busier now than before I left for dinner. It wasn't full, but it was close. As I got my change back from Chase, I could see a folded envelope included with it. I shoved it in my pocket and thanked her as I walked towards the door that said pool.

I entered to find a couple of pool tables and an outside seating area. I sat at a table and looked around while lighting a cigarette. A couple of guys played a game of pool on the far table, and a group of ladies doing the same closest to me. I sat down and pulled the note from my pocket. As I opened it, I saw the phone number first, then a note.

If you're here all week, let's grab a drink together. C x

Why not? As the night went on, and in-between Chase serving customers and glass collecting, I arranged to meet her tomorrow after work for dinner and a few drinks. I then said goodnight and left.

Once I was back in the hotel room, I lay on the bed, and my thoughts began spiralling again. I put both my hands over my eyes as images began to speed across my mind. As I was slowly falling asleep, I became excited about my date with Chase. My mind flashed to how Roberts head had looked. I adjusted my pillows and slowly drifted off

The next day, I walked around smiling to myself and praying there would be no delays in work. I was really looking forward to tonight. The workday was finished by four that afternoon, and the machine was "LIVE", so once again, I was able to go early.

I pulled up outside my hotel and called Chase, who was off today. She told me she would meet me in the hotel and decide together on where to go for dinner and drinks. This worked for me, I told her. I let her know I would be about 20 minutes because I would take a quick shower and tidy myself up a little. As I got out of the shower and dried myself off, I heard a gentle knocking on the hotel door. I wrapped the towel around my midriff and secured it as I walked to the door and opened it. It was Chase; she had come early. There were two grocery bags in her hands. I grabbed them from her quickly and said. "Hi, come in; I'm nearly ready, just going to put some clothes on." As I put the bags on the floor by the dressing table, I turned around, as she had just closed the hotel door. I could see she had on a flowery summer dress and sandals. The dress wasn't a bright yellow but a subtle shade. She looked different than she had the previous night, more relaxed, refreshed even.

"How has your day been?" I asked her.

"Oh, it's been ok; it's about to become better." With this, she lunged towards me, knocking me onto the bed. Then she dropped down onto the bed and pulled my towel off of me. We fucked for half the night. Chase was dirty. She liked it anyway, and I was prepared to try. We satisfied both our needs. We had snacks for food, and Chase had beers in the grocery bags. Chase stood out the front and smoked a joint before coming back into the hotel and doing more things to my body. We eventually fell asleep on top of the bed.

I woke up early to find Chase already dressed and heading out the door. I said, "I'll call you later after work."

For a mere second, she stopped and, before she exited, turned to me and said, "I'll be in work tonight. I'm on six till closing," as she closed the room door and was gone.

I went about my day as usual. We ended up being delayed in going "LIVE" today as we waited for a part to be delivered from a warehouse in Palm Springs. It was gone seven before I walked into Chase's bar for a quick beer. I was worn out and could feel that today was catching up with me. Chase had worn me out last night, and today work had been a right ball ache. As I walked in, Chase put a Coors on the bar and smiled at me. Like the previous evening, the bar began to slowly fill up with people because there was a pool tournament. Chase had blown me off when I tried to talk to her tonight. I figured she was busy with the pool tournament. As I headed into the restroom, she followed me in. "Hey Will, about last night, you know it was just sex, right?" I laughed as I zipped my jeans up and began washing my hands.

"Of course, Chase. I was only polite."

"No problem," she said. "I'm glad we got that sorted out," and left the restroom. Tameka only wanted a fuck buddy, too drifted across my mind.

"Californian girls," I said and laughed loudly at my bad sense of humour. It was nearly 9 pm, and I was ready to call it a night. I got up to leave, and as I did, a woman walked through the door. She was bleach blonde, about 5ft 9, wearing a black leather jacket and a pair of faded jeans. Underneath, there was a black Rolling Stones t-shirt and a pair of matching black suede ankle boots. I looked into her eyes as she pulled her jacket off and sat in the seat next to me in the only seat left at the bar. She had sparkling blue eyes, and her body was shaped perfectly. I smiled as she sat next to me.

"Coors Light," she said to Chase. Chase already knew her.

"Good evening, Madison," she greeted as she placed a bottle in front of her.

After she had taken a sip, she looked at me and said, "I don't think I've seen you in here before," and smiled.

"Yeah, I'm a newbie, but don't tell anyone," and smiled back as I sat back on my seat. Madison and I seemed to talk constantly; we went round for round, as Madison wouldn't allow a man to pay for her. She was working, so she pays her own way. Before long, it was nearly midnight. I asked Chase for the tab and settled up. She had been looking at me funny all night. I let Madison know I was leaving because I had to be up early for work

As I stood up, she asked me, "Will you be here tomorrow night, Will?" I could get lost in those eyes, I thought.

"Yeah, more than likely, Madison."

"I might see you then," she said and smiled again at me. Madison was stunning. The conversations we had could have lasted for hours. Madison was a happy daydreamer, just like myself. I had a really nice time and felt completely at ease. I gave Madison a little hug and said goodbye.

As I walked into my hotel room, my phone started to beep. I had three messages from Chase. The messages were an attempt to warn me from having anything to do with Madison. It was obvious from reading them Chase had no time for Madison. I didn't respond, having no time to indulge in Chase's paranoia. As I lay falling asleep, I thought about Madison and the way she had held herself. There was no denying it; she turned me on. She was a confident woman who, like me, knew what she wanted from life. I had heard earlier in the evening how she works for her father in a trucking business. One day, the business would become hers in the future, but it was clear from just one conversation with her that she was destined for greater things. My mind began to drift again. I started to think about Drew and her husband. Weirdly, I thought about the goldfish Cameron had and how the water from its bowl splashed everywhere on the drive to Joe's. I was gone again.

The alarm woke me the following morning, and, in a flash, the day just flew by. It made up for the ball ache of the previous day. I went back to the hotel to freshen up and sent a few work emails before heading to the bar.

One more workday is left this week. I sat in the same seat as the night before. Chase wasn't working tonight; it was the red-haired woman who had worked the previous night during the tournament. Chase had messaged me about four times throughout the day, attempting to warn me about Madison. About eight that evening, Madison showed up. As soon as she entered, she walked toward me. She had a pair of white knee-length shorts on, a yellow tank top, and matching sandals. I could see the thong she had on as she sat in the seat next to me. Madison put her bag on the floor. It was then I saw she had a small red devil tattooed holding a pitchfork above her left ankle. Madison reached in and kissed me on the cheek.

"Good evening, Will. How was your day?" She rubbed the side of my cheek to remove the lipstick from her kiss.

"Fine, thanks, Madison. It flew by." I said while shouting in for a few beers. We sat talking about each other's days. Madison listened to me, showing genuine interest in how my day had been. She explains how one of her father's drivers had crashed a truck today worth over a hundred thousand dollars. Her father was fuming. The night was going exactly as the previous night had gone.

By ten that evening, Madison said, "Let's get out of here, Will. Your hotel or my place?"

I laughed as I shrugged my shoulders. We ended up back in my hotel room. We didn't fuck, but we connected. The intimacy was as strong as it had been with Tameka. We enjoyed each other's bodies. I enjoyed spending the night with Madison and somewhat wished it would never come to an end. I don't recall falling asleep that evening. We did, however, sleep past the alarm clock the following morning. I have never done that before, priding myself on always being on time.

I was only twenty minutes late and blamed it on a crash at the intersection by my hotel. Of course, no such incident had occurred. In a rush to leave in the morning, I had to leave Madison in the hotel room. As I drove to the bank, I thought about how good she looked in the morning. I could have stayed in bed all day with her. She showed up at the bank I was working at just before lunch. I had left my wallet on the dresser during my hasty exit a few hours earlier. I arranged to see her next week on Monday, being not too far away in Beaumont and Banning again for the next week. Madison invited me over to her place for dinner on Monday after we had both finished work. I thanked her and told her, "I'll look forward to it." I was having little surges of rushing in my stomach as she walked away from me. I knew this was excitement, joy, happiness, or a combination of all three. It was clear that Madison was affecting me.

I finished work, grabbed a six-pack of Coors, and went back to the hotel for an early night. I want an early start tomorrow morning to be as fresh as possible for my weekend. I was already lying down on the bed when Chase texted me and asked if it was ok to stop by after she finished work at 2 am. I apologised and said, "I can't as I'm up and out first thing." I didn't hear from her again. I sent Madison a quick text to say thank you for dropping my wallet off today. This led to us texting back and forth for a short time before saying goodnight and putting my phone on the side next to the bed. I couldn't stop thinking about the previous night. I could feel myself drifting away, losing myself in thought about another night with Madison.

I was up and out the following morning, and just after 1 pm was pulling up at home. I had taken to driving the truck everywhere now. I hadn't used my own truck in a while. I had let Kristen borrow it, but she never returned it. We spent the weekend clubbing it as we usually did. Cameron made out with Roland outside the club as we headed out to leave. Cameron insisted on how she wanted to go home with Roland, but Joe told her she's had too much to drink and wouldn't let her go. I backed

Joe up the second Cameron decided to argue in her defence. We know she really likes Roland but explained to her it couldn't happen like this. Joe managed to convinced Cameron, and we all drove home in the cab.

The remainder of the weekend was ordinary; I headed back to the hotel in Beaumont on Sunday morning. On my drive, Madison texted me and asked if I had arrived yet. I called her to let her know I had not long left, and we discussed the dinner that she was going to cook tomorrow evening. I spent the evening on my laptop doing work schedules and responding to emails still unanswered from the previous week. I let Bernard know how things had been going, like a monthly report thing, but nothing formal. I put my last cigarette out at 10.16 pm that evening. My mind had its own mission tonight and couldn't control its path. The train of thoughts had become random. From Daryl's weight to Cameron's naked body to Drew, then to the mess Robert's head made. I could feel myself going as I drifted into my dreams.

A light tapping on the hotel door woke me up. It startled me at first because it was so dark and disorientating in the room. I looked at the clock on the dressing table; it was 3.12 am. I jumped up out of bed and looked out of the peephole in the door. It was Chase. I opened the door, and as soon as I did, Chase began falling onto my chest. I could smell the alcohol. She was drunk. I managed to stand her up off me as she swayed. "Did I wake you?" slurred out her lips as she pushed past me and dropped her handbag to the floor, and fell face-first onto the bed. I closed the hotel door and switched on the light. I tried talking to Chase repeatedly, but she was too far out of it to comprehend anything I was saying. What she did manage to say in response was just gibberish and impossible to understand. As I stood there looking at Chase, my mind began thinking out loud. You're going to be my first, well, my first that I have planned. I was excited. My stomach began rushing. My breathing was becoming heavier; my heart started pounding in my chest. A warmth spread throughout my whole body. I pulled the seat out by the dressing table and sat in it. I lighted a cigarette and stared at Chase as she slept.

"She just won't wake up," I said out loud. "No one knows she's here." My first thought was I'm going to strangle her, but I decided to smother her with a pillow instead. I got up and rolled Chase over, so she was now lying on her back, facing upwards. Her eyes were closed; she was completely out of it. The smell of alcohol was sickly sweet. She didn't move or even stare as I covered her body with the duvet. I stood and looked at Chase one last time. Sealing her under the duvet, I climbed on top of her body and pulled a pillow from the side of the bed. I pushed the pillow hard onto her face and leaned forwards as if to shift my weight onto it. For roughly ten to fifteen seconds, she didn't even budge, absolutely nothing, but then she started kicking her legs and struggling with all her might in a feeble attempt to escape. I pushed harder on the pillow. Chase fought for minutes. So much that when she did finally stop struggling, my body felt like I had just done a workout.

I was completely drained. I pulled the pillow free of her face. Her eyes were closed, and she looked a pale shade of blue. Her mouth had drool coming out the side that rolled down her cheek onto the bedsheets. I went and sat back in the seat by the dressing table and lit up another cigarette. I have to be at work at 9 am this morning. As I looked towards the clock, I saw it blinking at the time of 4.22 am. Fucking Chase! Now I'm not going to get any sleep. My mind went straight to work. This wasn't the first time I had cleaned up, and it wouldn't be the last, I thought. I moved fast; by 5 am Chase was cleaned, wrapped in plastic, and already loaded into the back of the truck.

I went back to the hotel room and got showered myself. I bagged up all her clothes and handbag. I emptied her purse out into the bag of clothes and pulled her driving license-free. I read Chase Baker, 28. The address on it was local, in Beaumont. I dropped it into the bag and tied it up. I had seen a place locally that had huge dumpsters outside it, and it was off an alley, so I would be able to do this without being seen.

I left quickly, as the day was already beginning to start. I drove the truck down the alleyway quietly; dawn had already broken by now. I stopped the truck and quietly got out and opened the back. I pulled the roll of plastic that she was wrapped in out the truck and placed it down to the side of the dumpster. I unrolled Chase's naked body out of the plastic and put the plastic back in the truck. I closed the truck quietly and looked at Chase once more quickly as her body lay naked on the concrete. I got back in the driver's seat of the truck and went back to the hotel for breakfast.

At the breakfast table, I acted as if everything was normal. Madison texted me to see how I had slept. That was nice of her, I thought, and replied with, yes, I had a good sleep. I set about my workday without a care in the world. As soon as I finished, I called Madison to let her know I was done for the day. We arranged for me to go over at 6 pm. This was perfect for me. I have time for a shower first.

Just after six, I pulled the truck up outside 1040 Jon Bell Avenue. The house was big, not as big as Joe's place, but still a very good size. I grabbed the red wine I had brought from Joe's wine cupboard and headed towards the door. Just as I was about to ring the doorbell, the door opened, and Madison stood there in a pair of demin shorts, a dark blue t-shirt, and pink fluffy slippers on her feet. "Come in," she said with a smile as she headed up the hallway. I closed the door and followed her in. I could smell garlic in the air. "I've made spaghetti Bolognese Will, please don't tell me you're a vegan?

"Hell, no. I love meat too much," I said. I put the wine down on the counter and then kissed Madison passionately. We sat at the kitchen table most of the evening, just chatting and eating. Madison had cooked the spaghetti sauce the previous day and explained that the recipe had been passed down from her grandma. We finished the food and then moved to the couch. We found it hard to keep our hands off each other as we caressed each other's bodies and made out on the couch.

"Do you want to stay?" she asked me as she was biting on my neck.

"Yes, of course, I do." She stood up, grabbed me by my hand excitingly, and directed me towards the bedroom. Being in her own home, Madison was more enjoyable. We could spend five minutes together or twenty-four hours, and it would still feel as if only a few seconds had gone by.

10

TESS SAUNDERS & JOSE RAMIREZ

On Sunday, I did not leave for work until after lunchtime. For over an hour, I sat on the 10 freeway just outside Nicklin. Traffic was moving, but not fast enough. I decided to pull off in the next town of Cherry Valley to grab a soda and cool down. I took the exit and continued up the road I had taken before working at the Cherry Valley Bank. I could see the 7-11 sign up ahead, a convenience store that sells everything from beer to cakes to newspapers.

As I drove the truck into the 7-11 parking lot, it dawned on me how small it was for my huge trick. This had happened a lot of times before. I did my usual improvising and found a parking spot where I would not block anyone in or prevent exit or entrance, but this was very difficult. I drove past the 7-11 and parked right up on the side of the building, blocking the trash dumpsters. I jumped out to run in to grab some cigarettes, a six-pack for the hotel, and a soda to drink for the rest of the journey. As I headed back towards the truck's tail end, I could see the outline of a shadow moving. As I passed the first dumpster, I noticed a guy stand up as if he had been sitting down on the side of the second dumpster. He was only small, maybe 5ft 4 and his head was completely shaven. Only when his head lifted could I see he had a large moustache above his lips. He wore dark blue baggy jeans, white sneakers, and a white t-shirt that had to be three times the size he needed. He was covered in tattoos all over his arms, neck, and even on his face below his left eye.

As I was about to pass him, he stepped back. We didn't make eye contact. Before I even saw him move, he's pulled a gun from the beltline of his jeans. The gun rears up, so it points towards my face. "WOW," I heard myself saying, as I was shocked.

"Give me ya fucking wallet, pendejo."

I responded instantly. "Ok, ok, keep cool, my man," as I started to reach for my wallet.

"SLOWLY, motherfucker," he shouted as he waved the gun around in my face. My stomach had dropped.

I answered him very quickly. "SORRY, mate, it's all good. You can take the wallet." My hand reached into my back pocket. The next few seconds happened in a flash. As I had finished saying he could take the wallet, his shoulders dropped down as if he became relaxed. He looked away for a split moment to check there wasn't anybody watching. I raised my wallet, and he snatched it.

"I want the watch too, pendejo," he said, waving the gun round in my face. As I reach for the watch to take it off, he steps sideways as if he's anxious and quickly looks around. I saw my hand moving, but before I realised I had connected a punch to the side of his head. It was as if a fuse had blown in my head. He staggered backwards, and I erupted without a moment of haste. I was on him. I hit him repeatedly. This time the gun dropped to the floor and he bounced off the wall of the 711. Who the fuck does this guy think he is? My mind was controlling my body as I hit him again. The guy dropped to the floor and stopped moving; he was out cold. The adrenaline had kicked in. My heart was pounding in my chest; I launched forward and stamped twice on the back of his head.

"I'm the wrong fucking guy to fuck with," I said. I leaned over and picked my wallet up, slipping it back in my pocket. I headed towards the back of the truck. I knew what was going to happen next. I saw the gun just behind the rear wheel of the truck. It had landed there as he dropped it. I picked it up quickly and placed it under my shirt. I opened the back of the truck. I went back and picked him up. I draped him over my shoulder and threw him like a rag doll in the back of the truck. He groaned as he landed. I climbed in and closed the door. I proceeded to tie him up with an extension cord. I grabbed a washrag from my supplies, shoved it in his mouth, and used duct tape around his head to keep the rag steady. I didn't cover his nose; however, the thought had occurred to me. I want to have some fun by teaching this fucker a lesson. I made sure he was secure and jumped out of the truck. I lit up a cigarette and climbed back into the driver's seat, opening the window.

Back on the freeway, I got out of there as quickly as possible. This week, I was heading for the Town of Palm Springs. I had passed a place or two around those areas on my journeys back and forth over the last few years. There were a few places in the area that were, shall we say, secluded and quiet. I exited the freeway in Cabazon and headed up the Milard Pass Road. It wasn't a road as in the tarmac kind, but just a line of dirt that went right into the desert and surrounding mountains.

I pulled up on the side of the road once the truck was no longer visible to the surrounding area. I jumped out and headed towards the back. As the back rolled upwards, I saw the guy had woken up and was looking right at me. I could see the fear in his eyes. I smiled at him. "It's no good being scared now." I climbed in the truck and dragged him along his belly towards the opening. I left him there to grab a shovel from my tools in the corner. I spent the next two hours digging in the heat of the sun. I thought about Madison quite a bit. I was meeting up with her as much as possible. I loved her company as much as I did with Joe and Cameron. When the hole was finally ready, I grabbed a bottle of Coors, lit a cigarette, and rested for a short while on the side of a huge boulder. Once I had cooled myself down a little in the heat, I picked my bottle up and climbed back into the truck. I searched the guy, but he had nothing on him; well, seventy-six cents in change in one of his pockets. I looked him right in his eyes as he lay there, looking terrified. "I will speak. You will listen, blink to let me know you understand me." He blinked his eyes towards me. I pulled the rag out of his mouth. "What is your name?" I asked him.

"José Ramirez," he said fast. "Please, please, don't hurt me. I have two little girls." I pushed the rag back into his mouth, then dragged him forward and dropped him out the back of the truck. He yelped as he landed on the rocky terrain. I jumped down and dragged him to the hole, pushing him in.

"You should have thought about that first, Jose.; this time, you chose the wrong person to rob." I grabbed my shovel and began putting the sand back in. I watched him as he groaned and squirmed, but eventually, he could no longer move. The weight of the sand had him trapped. I thought about grabbing the gun and burying it with him. However, I realising it might be good to have for emergencies. I looked Jose right in the face and threw the remaining soil over the top of his face. I didn't feel anything at all for Jose. I could have shot him or beat him with the shovel, which would have been the more humane thing to do, but a part of me figured this is what he deserved. I cleaned up and headed back towards the freeway.

Next stop, Palm Springs. I checked into the hotel and later that evening talked with both Joe and Cameron on the phone. Joe asked if we could all go out for dinner this Friday because there was a new restaurant he wanted to try out in LA. We agreed as long as we could hit the club afterwards.

The work week went by quickly; I spent most evenings with Madison, as she lived so close to Palm Springs. I spent a few nights over at her place. As it was my last day of work in the area tomorrow, I arranged to meet Madison at the bar for a few drinks later that evening. Come that evening, we ended up back at Madison's place. The house had the view at the rear across a golf course and we could watch the sunset. The property alone had to be worth a million. Her parents had given Madison the place. They had bought a huge place in Banning the next town over. Although the house was big, Madison only lived in the kitchen, bedroom area, and TV room. The breeze would come across the golf course on a hot day and come right through the patio doors, keeping the room cooler. It was as if I had two separate lives now: the one where I'm out clubbing with my friends and having fun all weekend, and then there's the work-life, in which I was enjoying killing people.

Where does Madison come into this? My mind drifted towards thinking about her and how I felt around her. As I drifted to sleep that night Madison lay on my chest and the smell of her hair made me think of a summer day.

Before I knew it, the week was over, and I was walking out onto the patio at home, and Cameron was hugging me. "I'll be glad to get this restaurant out of the way tonight, Cam. Joe hasn't shut up about it all week. Every time I've spoken to him, it's are you still coming out Friday night to try the restaurant. I'm not even fussed about sushi."

Cameron smiled at me and said, "Yeah, he's super excited, isn't he," and we began chuckling to ourselves. Cameron and I fooled about in the pool for a while. Just after four that afternoon, Joe showed up. He was made up to see me; I really missed these two. Joe told me how Cameron had done a ladies' night on Wednesday evening and how he come round on Thursday morning to a room of half-naked bodies in underwear running about. Joe's version of the story was a lot funnier than my version. We sat at our patio table, drinking Coors, and caught up with one another on how the weeks had gone. Joe finished his beer and put the bottle in the trash.

"I've ordered us a town car to and from the restaurant, guys. It will be here by seven," Joe informed us as he walked in to get ready. By seven that evening, the temperature was slowly dropping; Joe and I sat in the car as Cameron did the final touches to her makeup. We got to the restaurant fifteen minutes earlier than Joe had reserved the table for. He had been glued to his phone in the car all the way there, typing away like crazy.

"You going to be on the phone all night, Joe?" asked Cameron.

"Sorry, Cam, just sent my last text," he replied as he slips the phone into his pocket.

"Mr Dicorpo, your table is ready," said the hostess as she proceeded to show us to our seats. The restaurant was packed, even the bar area was standing room only. Once we all got settled in our chairs. Joe began talking.

"Guys, I've asked you here today for a reason, and it isn't just to try the food." I look towards Cameron as she looks towards me.

"Intriguing, Joseph" Cam responded.

Joe carried on. "You're both my best friends or, as Will would say, best mates." Cameron and I laughed at this as Joe continued. "I have met someone." He paused as if he was observing our faces for a reaction. "Her name is Tess. We have been somewhat seeing each other casually for a little while, but with no strings. We are becoming attached. We have decided to let our feelings flow and try to give it a go. We both really like each other and guys, I feel different when I'm around her," Joe finished and stared towards us both.

"What?" Cameron said as she smiled. "That's why you have been glued to your phone."

I responded. "Awesome Joe, do we know her?"

"No, Will. It's a woman who I met through a client."

"When do we get to meet her then, Joseph?" Cameron asked.

"Tonight, my dear Cam, tonight. She is just getting out of a taxi now." We all looked at each other in a bit of shock.

"Ok. Let's get this meet and greet out of the way," I said with a grin and looked at Cameron, who still had a surprised look on her face. Joe stood to meet Tess as she approached, as did I. Cameron remained seated. Tess walked towards Joe and kissed him on the lips.

"Tess, this is Will and Cameron. These two are not only my best friends, but the people I love the most," Joe said. I looked at

Tess as Cameron greeted her with a small hug and a smile. Tess was in her late 30s and Asian American. She had lovely long black hair that reached down to her waist tied up in a ponytail. She was wearing a small black outfit that showed all the curves of her body shape. She wasn't very tall, even in high heels, possibly 5ft 4 at a push. She had dark brown eyes, and you could see she has had a boob job. They were eye-catching, so much so it was hard not to look. I'm not saying they look huge like Pamela Anderson, but you could see she had work done on them along with her face.

"Nice to meet you, Will. I've heard so much about you," as she stepped in close to me and gave me a peck on the check. She hugged me and stepped back towards Joe. Cameron greeted Tess, and as they exchanged pleasantries, Joe helped Tess to her seat and gave her a little smile as he sat down. Cameron looked at me as if she was trying to read my mind. I just gave her a little smile back as if to say, "let's see." We ordered two bottles of wine right away. By the time they had gone, we were all talking freely. Tess had met Joe through one of his clients, whom they shared but provided different services. They had been seeing each other off and on for nearly a year. How didn't we know about this?

I gazed towards Joe and listened. Tess told us how she was originally from Pennsylvania and had moved out to California after university to take a position in ATREK. The company ATREK was one of the biggest alcoholic suppliers in the states, if not the whole world. We heard how her parents had settled in Pennsylvania after migrating from Korea in the 70s. Tess appeared to be a lovely woman. It was obvious why Joe had taken a shine to her. Cameron asked Tess a load of questions at first, but she lay off as the evening went by. When we had finished eating, Joe asked Tess if she would like to come back for a drink, and she agreed.

We all sat on the patio, looking out towards the night. We were still talking as the sun was rising over Los Angeles. I headed to bed first, and within a few minutes, I heard Joe and Tess in the corridor entering his room. My door opened; it was Cameron. She asked me if I was still awake.

"Yes, Cam," I said. She closed the door and climbed into bed next to me.

"What do you think about Tess?" she asked in an inquisitive voice.

"What do you think?" I said as my answer.

She said, "I like her; she makes Joe happy you can see it on his face."

"I agree, Cameron. She is perfect for Joe," I replied. We lay chatting quietly about the evening until I was fast asleep. The last thing I heard from Cameron was how warm my chest was as she lay on it.

The next day we spent around the pool. Joe and Tess were all lovey-dovey towards each other. In the early afternoon, Jess and Kristen showed up. I lay on my chest on a sun lounger, sunbathing and watching them playing in the pool. Joe joined me later on because the girls were messing around in the pool.

"Hey bud, I didn't get a chance last night with everything that's going on. What do you think of Tess?" he asked, and looked directly at me, waiting for an answer.

"I love her, Joe. She makes you happy, and that's the main thing to me. Do you love her, mate?" I said.

"I think so, Will. I'm pretty sure I do. I can't stop thinking about her. If I'm not with her, I want to be, Will," and he smiled towards me. I got up and hugged him. It was a nice feeling seeing Joe this happy.

Tess shouted over to us from the pool, "Get a room, will you? We don't want to see that."

We all started laughing as Joe said to me quietly, "I'm glad you like her, and I think Cameron does too. I'm debating asking her to move in. What do you think?" he asked.

"It's your house, Joe; so, it's your decision, mate," I responded with a smile.

"Thanks, Will. You are a good man." I smiled as I thought

about the struggle Drew had given. We spent the rest of the night just relaxing and chatting. Jess was becoming her usual drunken self. I used this as an excuse to escape for the night. I said goodnight to everyone and headed to bed. As I slipped away, I thought about Madison. I hadn't said anything to Joe or Cameron about her. Why not? Am I keeping her as my secret? They're my best friends, but I haven't said anything to them about her. I haven't even so much as mentioned the name Madison.

11

TODD AND LAURA & ROLAND RODRIGUEZ

La Quinta, CA. I had never heard of the place. I had to get someone to say it to me a few times to learn how to pronounce it myself. The town wasn't very big, consisting of a shopping mall, a few bars, and restaurants all along a bustling high street. There was only one bank in the area, and this had two ATMs.

My first day flew by, and the machine was up and "LIVE" just before three that afternoon. There wasn't much in the tiny town of La Quinta. I found a sports bar called "The Beer Hunter" in a small plaza situated next to my hotel. As I walked in, I could see people eating at a table to my left. Perfect, beer and food, I thought. The bar wasn't dark like most bars in the little towns I had visited but was relatively bright and airy. I sat at the bar next to a couple who had their heads buried in a menu. I ordered a Coors from the bartender presented to me by a gentleman in his late 40s with a tremendous beard. It was so long it was the first thing anyone would have noticed about him.

The bartender stood as tall as me but was not as broad in the shoulders. His hair was also long and tied into a short ponytail at the back of his lower neckline. I paid for my beer, grabbed a menu off the bar, and headed towards a booth area in the back. I sat on the bench and got comfy. The couple from the bar, who were both in their late 40s, sat in a booth directly opposite from me.

The husband was dressed in a light grey suit with a white shirt and a black tie. On his feet, he wore black leather shoes. His hair was short and combed over to one side; his face was partially obscured by a pair of black-framed glasses on his shaved face.

Presumably, his wife was sitting across from him and wearing a tight black dress revealing in the front with a pair of matching black leather high-heels. Her hair was a dark brown and straight, just short of her shoulders. The two of them looked casually smart. I watched them from over my phone as they talked back and forth. Now and then, I would catch the lady playing footsie with him under the table.

As I had finished my second beer and began to light a cigarette, the lady at the booth across from me looked at me, got up, and heading towards me.

"Do you have a light, please?" she said with a smile.

"Yeah, sure, Hun." She leaned in with her cigarette. The usual question fell from her mouth "Are you English?". I respond in my typical fashion, and we talk for a few minutes back and forth from our booths until the guy asks if it's ok for them to join me.

"Yeah, sure. The more, the merrier," I said and smiled. They both joined me at my booth and sat across from me at the table.

"I'm Todd, and this is my wife, Laura," as they both shook my hand.

"I'm Will. Nice to meet you both."

Todd ordered a round of drinks in, and we sat talking. I heard how Todd was a semi-pro golf player and spent all his time on the golf course practising. Laura was the typical housewife who stayed home and cleaned. I listened to how excited she became when she was describing her book club meetings every second Monday. How quiet life must be living in a small town, I thought to myself. Todd was on his phone for the entire evening. I mainly chatted with Laura. We talked about a lot of things, and Todd would join in when he was at the table. We ended up staying till gone midnight. I said goodbye and left for the hotel. I was happily buzzed and dropped off to sleep quickly that evening.

The next day was hot; it was 112 degrees. I was melting in the sun all day.

At four in the afternoon, I walked back into "The Beer Hunter" and sat at the bar with the day behind me. On the previous day, the gentleman who had served me said, "Coors?" to me as he reached into the refrigerator.

"Yes, please," I said with a smile. Suddenly, as he was putting the bottle on the bar, my eyes were covered. I could feel the soft skin of the fingers as they wrapped across my face.

"GUESS WHO?" I heard from behind me in a female voice. I knew instantly by the voice it was Laura who I had met the previous evening.

"It's Laura," I said as she released my eyes and put her arm around my shoulders as if to hug me from behind.

"Hey Will, come and join me," she said. "I'm all alone today," and pointed towards a booth. I grabbed my bottle and told her to lead the way.

Today Laura was wearing a dark grey skirt, a white blouse, and white high heels. She looked as if she had just left a business meeting. We sat in the window that looked out across the parking lot. "Todd's on his way," she said. "He's running late." She clicked her phone on the table.

"How has your day been, Hun?" I asked Laura. She smiled back at me with a dreamy look.

"I love the way your accent sounds; it's just so bloody sexy," she replied. I laughed, a little embarrassed, to be honest. I had never had an older woman look at me like this before. We talked for a little about mostly nothing, and then Todd showed up.

Todd was wearing his golfing clothes. He had on a pair of beige shorts, a navy polo shirt, and shoes that looked as if they were speciality golf shoes if such things even existed. He joined us at the table.

We had some food that Laura ordered and drank a few beers. Come seven that evening, I was half shot and was starting to feel it. Laura went to the restroom, and as she did, Todd began to talk to me.

"Do you know Will I have been married to Laura for fifteen years now? As each day goes by, I love her more. We are perfect together. What I'm about to say next is private." He lowered his voice slightly. "Laura likes to have the occasional other man from time to time. I am, however, perfectly happy about this and even encourage her. You only live once, Will. Would this be anything you're interested in by chance?"

"What as in wife sharing? Or, you want me to share your wife?" I responded quite sharply with confusion. He looked me directly in the face.

"I want you to fuck Laura while I watch," he said. I looked at him, and it was obvious from his face he was serious. At that point, Laura had returned from the restroom and sat back in her seat. Todd smiled at her and said, "I've asked him already. He hasn't responded yet, though." I looked back at him and then across to Laura. Our eyes connected; she said, "What do you think, Will? One night, no strings attached?" she asked in a curious but welcoming voice.

"Of course, why not?" I heard myself say. Laura and Todd both smiled at me. We finished our drinks, settled the bill, and left. Todd told us he was going to walk ahead and get things ready. Laura and I walked across the parking lot. We watched as Todd crossed the street and went into a caravan park before disappearing around a corner.

"Ok, Will, let me explain the dynamics to you," she said. "Todd likes to watch, but it's more than that."

I interrupted her immediately. "I don't go both ways."

She laughed loudly and then said, "NO, it's nothing like that. You see, Todd likes to be humiliated and treated as if he's worthless and nothing. I tie him up and ball gag him as he lays there and watches another man take what is his. It sounds strange, but we have been doing this for ten years now. Todd gets what he wants out of this relationship, and I get to have sex with as many men as I like. And I like you, Will," she finished and smiled towards me.

I know a lot of people would have been gone in a heartbeat. I wasn't bothered. I always have believed each to their own when it comes to the bedroom. I knew two lads in Redbank that were constantly getting caught in a cell together. It doesn't bother me. Straight, gay, lesbian; whatever tickles your boat. As long as you're not hurting anyone who cares, isn't life for the living? These two found the thing they both like to do. I heard that Todd wants to be tied up, making him mine, as easy as shooting fish in a barrel.

At the bottom of the road, we came to the last caravan on the left. It wasn't pitch black yet, but it was very close. The nearest light was fifty meters away at the top of the road. I followed Laura in and immediately noticed Todd standing nearly naked. He had on a black leather thong, and his head was covered by a gimp mask. It was also leather; it had two eye holes and a zip across the mouth area. My initial thought, at first sight, was, "this is bizarre".

The caravan wasn't too big. As we entered, we were in the kitchen area, which had two doors leading off it to the right. There was a small living area that had a wraparound couch in it spread across three walls to the far left. There was a table and two benches that were attached to the wall in between the kitchen and living room. Overall, it was a cosy home, if a little cramped.

Laura passed me a drink. After which, she pretty much took over from there. She demanded Todd get on his knees as she spat in his face and slapped him. I watched as she walked to a cupboard and pulled out a large suitcase. Laura began struggling to lift it on the table, so I helped her and then stepped back. As Laura opened it, I could see it was full of sex toys. Chains, ropes and whips. Most of the stuff I have never seen before in my life. Laura hogtied Todd on the couch, all the time slapping him and calling him worthless and vile. I could see how they both enjoyed playing their parts, Laura just as much as Todd. Once he was hogtied, she opened the zip on his mask and forced a ball gag into his mouth. I heard his teeth catch it as she rammed it in. Once it was fully strapped, she stood up, turned to me, and said while biting her bottom lip, "I'm all yours, Will." I pulled her close and started kissing her. She gave in willingly and began kissing me back. I ripped her blouse open, exposing her cupped breasts in a black lace bra. Laura gasped and looked at me all innocently. I could see from her eyes that she wanted me.

"You're next," I said and pushed Laura back from me, releasing her from my hold. I walked to the suitcase on the table and looked in. I grabbed a pair of handcuffs out of the bag and walked towards her. I forcibly jerked her around, so her back was facing me. I handcuffed her hands behind her back. As I did, she gave out a gasp of excitement. I grabbed a gag from the case and put it in her mouth, and fastened it. I walked her to the couch that Todd lay on and sat her down next to him. I tied her ankles together tight and stood up to look at them both. I walked over to where Todd lay. He was still face down and in a hogtied position. I checked he was secure and couldn't escape, and then I lit up a cigarette. I sat at the table on the bench, facing them. As I looked at them, both staring back towards me, I began talking to them both.

"Well, well, look what we have now. You're both tied up and can't move. I'm going to finish you both this evening." I could see the instant fear come across their faces. The look coming from their eyes was shock and fear combined. They both began struggling and groaning all over the couch. "Be still," I barked towards them both. As they both stopped moving out of fear, I sat down and told them about my life in California. From when I first met Joe to how I met Drew and Christopher. I even mentioned the fucker Jose who tried to rob me. I could see the tears coming out of Laura's eyes as she sobbed repeatedly. I let her watch as I strangled Todd to death with a piece of rope from the suitcase.

I sat down, drank some of my beer, and lit up another smoke. I was becoming used to this now. I used the same rope from Todd to strangle Laura. Laura didn't struggle much. It was as if she knew it would be pointless and just succumbed to the idea of death.

When both were dead and lying on the couch, my mind kicked in. "Clean up, clean up," I heard my voice say out loud. This is going to be complicated. I can get them prepared and then drive the truck over and pick them up; that was my plan. I went in search of black bags. As I opened the cupboard under the sink in the kitchen area, I saw the black bags right next to the bottle of BBQ fuel. My thoughts changed quickly; I grabbed the BBQ fuel and went back towards their bodies. I dosed them both and the couch in the fuel and anything left I used on the remaining sections of the couch. Burn the fucking lot. A lot easier than trying to bring the truck to this caravan park. I found a bottle of paint remover in the cupboard that housed the broom and used that to douse the bedroom area. I lit a piece of paper and threw it on the bed. The whole room erupted in flames immediately; the bed had started burning, and fire began to leap up the walls. I walked towards the couches and threw a new piece on the sofa on the left. The fire rushed across. Both their bodies caught fire and went up in seconds. I grabbed my empty beer bottle and walked through the caravan door.

As I closed the door, I gave in and had one last look towards Laura's body. I saw the flames had engulfed her. I shut the door and made my way up the road towards the streetlight. I wasn't running, just in case this would draw attention or make a noise. As I left the caravan park and crossed the street back into the parking lot, I looked back in the direction and could see grey smoke coming from the area. As I turned into the hotel parking lot, I heard an explosion. It was like a bomb had gone off. I looked towards the caravan to see a fire cloud shaped like a mushroom coming up into the night sky. I walked into my hotel room and headed straight for the shower.

The next morning, I got up and headed towards Indio. We would be there all next week, so Bernard had scheduled us to do one bank today and another one next week.

Once the day was finished, come four that afternoon, I drove back to the hotel, tidied up, and checked out. I could have stayed another night, but I hadn't seen Madison this week and was sure she wouldn't mind me showing up. I texted Madison to let her know I would be there in the next hour. I didn't get a response. I figured she was still at work until 5 pm. I will be in Beaumont by 5.30, I thought and jumped on the freeway.

I turned into Madison's Avenue but couldn't see any parking big enough for the truck. I did notice a black Chevy Blazer parked right outside her house while Madison's car was parked further up the driveway. I looked for parking and saw a spot just across from Madison's in front of her neighbours. I drove to the end of the street, turned around, drove back up, and parked. As I did, my phone beeped, and it was Madison.

I'm at the bar. Meet me here

I put the truck into drive and pulled out. I looked at Madison's car as I went past, then saw a yellow snake decal on the back window of the Chevy Blazer and the writing "Don't tread on me" above it.

As I drove off, I somewhat recalled in my mind how that decal was military-related. I think they were the words the marines in the states use but I wasn't sure.

I got to the bar, but Madison wasn't there. I called her, and she answered right away. "Where are you?" she said before I had a chance to speak.

"I'm at the bar, Hun," I said.

She laughed and said, "I'm at home; I came straight back as soon as I got your text."

"No problem," I said. "I'll be with you in five."

"I'll leave the door open," she said as we hung up. As I pulled up outside Madison's, the Chevy Blazer had gone. I parked the truck and jumped out. Madison was in the shower when I went in and was just drying off when I walked into the bedroom.

"Want a beer, Hun?" I shouted to her through the door.

"Yes, please, babe. I won't be long," she responded. I went to the kitchen and opened two bottles. Madison came out in her dressing gown and greeted me. Feeling too lazy to cook, we ordered Pizza Hut that evening and had an early night. I was finished for the week, but Madison still had to work.

The following morning, Madison was up and out. I let her know I would call her over the weekend, as she kissed me and left. I had a coffee to get started and headed towards the warehouse.

Traffic in Los Angeles was a lot worse than it is in Beaumont, that's for sure. I didn't get back home until gone four that afternoon.

I arrived to find Cameron, Tess, Jess, Kristen, and a group of guys all swimming in the pool. I greeted the ladies, and they introduced me to the people I hadn't met before. The only guy I knew or had seen before was Roland. He was the guy Cameron had introduced me to in the nightclub. He's the one she likes. I put my shorts on and joined them on the patio. I found it cute watching Cameron roughhousing with Roland as he appeared to let her win. They looked happy with each other.

Just after six, as the sun was starting to set, Joe arrived home. We spent the rest of the evening as we did so often, drinking, chatting, and having a laugh. Roland's friends all left together, and it wasn't long after that Cameron headed off to her room with Roland. Tess and Joe went next. Tess wasn't living in the house full time but stayed over most nights. The house was in sync; we all worked well with each other. Somehow, we all just got on. It was obvious that Tess and Joe were moving along nicely, but it was even nicer to see the way Tess looked at Joe. She loved him and didn't care who knew it.

I sat and had another beer with Jess and Kristen before

heading to my room. I could hear them talking as they came into sleep in the front room. I lay awake for over an hour, replaying over and over what I had done to Todd and Laura. What was that explosion, I thought, gas bottle or something? That was damn loud, whatever it was. Then on to Drew and then right back to Daryl. I could hear Cameron in her room with Roland. I began to drift off, and my last thought was how happy my friends looked.

12

BERNARD SCHMITTS

My work week was nearly over again. I woke in my hotel room to the thoughts of us all dancing in the club last weekend. How Cameron and Kristen sexually danced with each other, and they knew that I was watching them. I dragged my feet to the floor and sat up, lighting a smoke. Today, I had Bernard coming in to visit me. He had sent me an email a few days before letting me know he would be arriving today. I got showered and ready and set off towards the bank.

As I pulled the truck into the bank's parking lot, I could see Bernard was already waiting for me. I knew he was due in today, but not so early. I parked up and jumped out. "Good morning, Will" said Bernard as he smiled towards me.

"Well, good morning to you Bern, how was the flight?" He grabbed my hand and pulled me in for a hug.

"It was fine, you know, long," he laughed.

"So, you're here to spy on me then? Some friend you turned out to be." I smiled as Bern quickly responded.

"Don't be so hasty, my dear, William, we can talk later," with a chuckle as he walked off towards the bank doors. I went about my day just like every other. Bernard was checked into the same hotel as me, so we arranged to go for dinner that evening. I could easily have been done by two that afternoon but slowed down to show Bern how precise and immaculate my work was—impressing the boss, a little per se. We laughed back and forth, discussing today's youth and how much the music has changed over the years.

That evening, we sat down and had dinner. Bernard was dressed for the occasion, wearing a light brown suit, white shirt, and a thin brown tie. He looked smartly dressed yet casual, right down to his dark brown shoes. I hadn't dressed the same. I had a tank top on, a pair of Bermuda shorts, and Adidas flip flops. As I sat across from Bernard, I said, "Hey, what's with the suit, Bern?" and laughed.

"Sorry, Will. I didn't have time to change." We laughed it off and had dinner. When we finished, we sat in the lounge drinking whiskey. I knew to pace myself here. This wasn't the first or second time I'd been drinking with Bernard. He had hollow legs; whiskey was no stranger to him.

We sat across from each other in two high back leather seats, and Bernard started talking. "Can I talk business with you for a few minutes, please, Will?" staring towards me, anticipating my response.

"Yeah, sure, Bern; why not? I'm dressed for it," and we both started laughing.

Bernard said, "I want to tell you a little about myself. When I left university, I was hired by Wincapa Bixdorf. I was twenty-one back then," he says with a smile. "I started at the bottom like everybody else but managed to work myself up. The reason I'm telling you all this is as I have a proposition to offer you; well, if you're interested," as he stared at me straight-faced.

"I'm listening, Bern, carry on," I responded in a curious tone.

"You see, Will. I knew when I got hired at Wincapa it was only a matter of time until I was running the place. I worked my way up through the ranks, working hard even on the weekends and over the Christmas holidays. Well, it's finally all paid off. I have been made a partner at the firm, Will. I'm no longer going to be in the field. I will now spend my days talking on the phone and having business meetings," I cut him short.

By interrupting him, "That's awesome news, Bern. Congratulations, well done," and shook his hand.

"Thanks, Will. That means a lot. Would you like to hear about my proposition now?"

"Well, of course, I do, Bernard. What are you thinking?" I said.

"Well, Will. You see, with me moving up and my assistant taking my position, I was wondering if you would like to start running the construction aspect for Wincapa. Initially, it will be in California, but once we move to another state, it will mean coming and hiring people like yourself to do your work. It will be your position to see they are trained and taught how to do what you're doing. Now, Will, this will require a lot more hours working and more travelling of course. It's ok if you decide it's too much and you can stay in the position, you're in with no problems at all. If you do, however, consider the position, it will also come with a pay raise. Anything you might be interested in, Will?" as he looked towards me, waiting for a response.

"Most definitely, Bern. Tell me more," I responded.

"I thought you might be interested, Will. Let me tell you more, see if this is something that could work for you. It would mean when we go out of state, you will be working 3 weeks straight out of the month. The last week you will be flown back to California for a week off, all paid for by the company, of course. It will, however, mean you're to stay in hotels for three weeks at a time now and conduct interviews with prospective contractors for each state. You're in charge of who we hire, so it's important you are confident in their work, or this will fall on you if they fail to GO LIVE on time. You will be given a company car for your home life and be picked up at each airport with a rental car. The company will supply you with a new credit card, and the salary to start is nearly double what you're paid now. $150 thousand per year."

"Damn," I interrupted Bern. "That's a lot of money, Bern."

"Yes, it is, Will, but it's also a lot more work." He told me about the medical package the company had come up with and how I would be covered in any state I was in at the time. I get eighteen paid days off each year, along with all national holidays like Christmas, New Year, etc. I had every bank holiday off anyway, as no banks were open on those days.

"Well, Will. I think I've explained the position as best I can. What do you think?" he asked and sat back in his seat, sipping on his drink.

"It all sounds very good, Bern. It really does. Can I have a few days to think about this? Give me a chance to run it by Joe and Cameron to see what they think, also," I quickly replied.

"Of course, Will. Take all the time you need. I will email you the proposal, plus the packages the company is offering. You have a look, talk it over with your friends, and let me know when you're ready to talk again; that sound good, Will?"

"Yes, Bern, that's perfect, thank you." We sat drinking whiskey until gone midnight. I listened to Bern's plans, for both of us, and Wincapa with interest. Once Bernard had finished talking, he said, "And with that, I'm going to bed." He stood up and smiled at me. I gulped my last drink down and stood up, too.

"Yeah, me too. Goodnight Bern," as I shook his hand and watched him go in the opposite direction to myself.

I lay on the bed smoking a cigarette when I got back to my room. I was going to ring Joe and Cameron to tell them my good news, but as I looked at the clock, it showed 12.46. I figured it was best not to wake them. I can tell them both tomorrow once I got home.

Usually, I would be up and out in the morning, but I had arranged to meet Bern for breakfast, which delayed me getting on the road.

As I was coming up to Beaumont, I pulled off. I wanted to pay a quick visit to Madison to tell her my good news. As I turned onto Madison's street, I didn't see her car in the driveway. She must have left for work already. I parked up outside and tried to call her, but she didn't answer. Maybe she was driving, I thought.

As I began to text her, I looked up from the driver's seat, and across the street, there was the same Chevy Blazer with the yellow snake decal on the back. He must live near here came across my mind as I sent the text to Madison.

Good morning. I'll call you tonight. x

I jumped back on the freeway and headed towards Los Angeles. I was feeling happy today. The sun was shining, and I was off for the weekend. I was content as I drove for nearly three hours back to the warehouse. I got unloaded and left to beat any traffic. Just before two that afternoon, I pulled up to the side of Joe's house. The house was quiet when I walked in. I looked around but didn't see anyone. I grabbed a cold beer from the fridge, pulled my shirt off, and stepped out into the heat on the patio. I sat at the table under the umbrella for about forty minutes when Cameron and Tess showed up.

"Hey girls, how's it going?" They both jumped on me to hug me.

"I do miss you, Will," said Cameron, as she squeezed me tighter before letting me go. For much of the afternoon, the three of us sat out the back drinking and mostly listening to Cameron talk about Roland. Once Joe made it home, we all did our weekly catch-ups and found out about each other's week. When it was my turn, I told the three of them what Bernard had offered me and about all the additional benefits that came with it: the salary and the car, etc. They all looked at me in shock. As if what I was saying was unbelievable.

"Well, what do you think?" as I stared between the three of them.

Joe said, "Oh my fucking god, Will. Well done!" and jumped towards me to give me a big hug, followed closely by Cameron and then Tess.

"I'm super happy for you," said Tess.

Cameron, who was still hugging me tightly, said, "This is AWESOME NEWS, Will," and as she was releasing me, whispered in my ear. "See, you have made it."

I kissed Cameron on the lips with excitement. Joe and Cameron went over the new contract that Bernard had emailed over to me that morning.

"This is an amazing offer, Will. It really is. I only make that much myself," he laughed. So, I'm now going to be making as much as Joe does. This made me smile.

After a lot of discussion between Joe and Cameron on the contract pros and cons, they both looked at me and said, "Take it, Will." I laughed at them all.

"What, you thought I wasn't? Does the contract look all correct guys, is everything in order?"

"Yes, babe," said Cameron. Joe nodded to agree with Cam. As I smiled towards the two of them, Cameron's phone rang. It was Kristen wanting the gate open so she could get in. Cameron took off through the house to click them in.

"Take a day or two to sleep on it, Will. See if anything comes into your mind against the job, and if nothing does tell Bernard, you'll take the position," said Joe as he walked towards me to grab my empty bottle off the table.

"I will, Joe, thank you, mate," as he affectionately squeezed my shoulder. Kristen and Jess showed up with some new vodka that had just come out for us to try. It was orange flavour. Roland showed up around an hour later, and we all sat about chilling in the warm evening drinking shots.

I was last to wake up the next day, and by the time I joined them all on the patio, the discussion was already fully underway. They had sat there talking about my job offer, going back and forth even more over my contract.

"Well, Will. What do you think? Take the job? Leave the job?" asked Cameron.

"I'm taking it, Cam," I responded and then began smiling.

"Well, that's all figured out then, Will," said Joe. That night we went to the club as usual. I ended up kissing Kristen at the end of the night drunk; well, we both were. Cameron and Roland left first because she was staying over at Roland's. We left Jess and

Kristen in the club as they wanted to carry on dancing while me, Joe, and Tess got a taxi home.

Before calling it a night, we stayed up and had a couple of beers on the patio. I lay in bed that night, knowing I'm now living the dream. I was excited, beyond happy, my life has changed again. I was gone.

I was woken up by raised voices and shouting coming from the hallway. I looked towards the clock. It was 2.41 in the morning. The sounds were loud but mostly muffled. Then I heard a scream. It was Cameron! I launched out of bed and into the corridor in the same breath. I could see Roland holding Cameron by the neck on the couch when I entered the living room. I ran over and pushed Roland onto the sofa beside Cameron. "What the FUCK are you doing?" I said. He ignored my question as if he hadn't heard me. He jumped right back at me and came towards me. I didn't hesitate or even take a moment to think. I was on him. I hit him three times before he even realised what was happening. He fell to the floor at Cameron's feet. I punched him again as he attempted to climb back to his feet. He was out cold.

"You ok, Cam?" I said as I pulled Cameron up from the couch and into my arms.

"Yes, babe. I'm fine; he just lost it. He was already drunk in the club but decided to carry on afterwards. He started becoming angry at me, so I made him bring me home."

Joe and Tess had heard all the noise and commotion now and entered the living room. Cameron explained what had happened; he accused her of looking at another man and then grabbed her arm to drag her to the car.

"When he got out of the car here, it became worse. He grabbed me by my neck and picked me up along the wall and threw me on the couch. I wasn't strong enough to stop him. Then you came out and got him to stop. This is the third time he's done this now. He gets drunk and blacks out."

Tess threw me the shorts she had gotten from my room. It was only then that I had realised I was completely naked. I apologised and slipped the shorts on quickly. This was an awkward position right now. Joe and Cameron had already seen me in action with Daryl and Robert, but Tess had no idea what monster lives under the same roof as her. We grabbed a few beers and sat down until Roland came around. He was very much disorientated and had no recollection of what had happened. Cameron explained what he had done to her, and he looked shocked like he didn't believe her. Joe helped him to the couch, and he sat down. I told him he was choking Cameron when I came in and how he came at me, leaving me with no option but to hit him. I apologised and explained how Cam was family to me. The night ended confusingly. I think Roland didn't believe what we had told him.

Cameron looked towards Roland. "You can't put your hands on me ever. I won't put up with that."

Joe immediately said, "If you put your hands on her again, I'm going to put my hands on you," and stared towards Roland.

He responded, "I don't know what I'm doing, Joe. I don't even remember driving here." Cameron pulled Roland into her arms and hugged him. "It's ok, and I know you didn't mean to hurt me. It's ok."

I went back to bed. I had to head back to work tomorrow. I said goodnight and left them in the living room. I lay on the bed and replayed the events in my mind to understand what had just happened. Had Roland blacked out from too much drink? Did I overreact by hitting him? Should I have just pushed him away again or held him? I knew that if anyone tried to hurt anyone close to me, they are mine.

I woke up late the next day, mainly as we had been woken up so late in the night. Cameron was already up and, in the kitchen, when I walked in.

"Good morning, babe," she said as she passed me my coffee.

"Good morning, Cam," I said, taking the coffee from her with a quick hug. Cameron and I sat on the patio drinking our coffees and talked. She had made Roland leave last night after things calmed down. She told me how scared she was of him and how he just flipped. She explained how he was his normal self, then once he drank some vodka at his place, he changed.

"It was as if I was dealing with Doctor Jekyll and Mr Hyde. He dragged me to the car, Will. I kept falling over my own feet, but he carried on dragging me. When he grabbed me by the neck in the hall, all I could do was scream. He is too strong for me to stop," she explained. "I can't be with a man like that, Will. Who knows, the next time he drinks, it could be worse. What would he have done if you hadn't stopped him, Will?"

She looked at me with worry in her eyes. "If it happens again, hun, let me know, and I'll take care of it. Ok?"

"I'm scared, Will. If he, does it again, Joe will snap. He's not calm like you, Will. He just snaps then there is no controlling him. He will end up in jail."

"Stop worrying, Cam. If it happens again, I will take care of it. I promise you there is nothing to worry about," as I smiled at her.

I sat and talked with Cameron until Tess and Joe finally resurfaced. Before I knew it, my bag was packed, and I was off again for another week. I called Bernard from the road to accept the position, and he told me he would get the ball rolling. Following my GPS to my next location, I drove down the 10-freeway thinking about how much my life would change again. I thought about how Roland was last night and how I had promised Cameron it would be ok. I hope this is the last time Roland gets that drunk. If it isn't, "I'll kill him", I said under my breath.

13

DAVID, WEBSTER & STACEY

Come March of 2003, and I was in the small desert town of Vista Santa Rosa. There were only two ATMs in this bank. On the second and final day in VSR, I noticed a man standing on the side of the bank's doorway. I only took notice of him because he was staring right at me. The guy started to approach me as if he was about to ask me a question. I stopped what I was doing and turned to meet him face to face.

"Are you from the UK?" he asked me.

I smiled and replied, "Yeah. I'm from sunny Liverpool, England."

"I thought I heard an accent," he said with a smile on his face.

He proceeded to tell me he has family in the UK – Swindon, to be exact. His accent made me double-check. I had to try to figure out in my mind what he had said. GOT IT. Of course, I have heard of Swindon. I had heard of a lot of towns and cities in the UK. I have, however, never visited Swindon and wouldn't even be able to point it out on a map if my life depended on it. We talked back and forth for a few minutes, in which I explained I had no idea where Swindon was and what I was doing over in California working at a Lincoln Cargo bank.

"I'm David," he said. I smiled and gently pushed his arm in an attempt to move him.

"David, you're blocking my sun," I chuckled. "I'm Will" it was then I saw the size of this man. David towered over me, but I somehow hadn't noticed this as we spoke until he was directly in between me and the shining sun. Looking at his face, I could see he was very young-looking. Guessing his age, I would say he was about 20, maybe 22, but not much older than that. His face was clean shaved with soft brown eyes, and his hair was short and tidy, combed over to one side. David was obviously on the football team in high school due to his size and weight alone. His calves looked like tree trunks and were as wide as my thighs. The best way I could think of to describe David was a boy trapped in a man's body. Meaning his body had matured quicker than his mind. The t-shirt he wore looked stretched out as if he had trouble pulling it on. I noticed he had a small tattoo on the inside of his right wrist. It was the initials ND and a badge or emblem above. He wore a faded grey pair of cargo shorts, the type with a million pockets in them and a pair of moccasins on his feet. You could see the creases in the heel as he had forced his feet into them without opening them first.

As I continued my work, David stood by talking to me for about twenty minutes. He told me how he and a few of his friends had taken to living off the grid and how they had all claimed some land just up the 10 freeway near the Patton memorial. How they all liked to party, drink beer, and smoke a few joints; he invited me to stop by if I wanted to have a drink and chill. I thanked him and said that I would think about it.

He responded. "Hey bro, we up there 24/7 swing in anytime. If you don't see my truck…" and he pointed across the parking lot to a black Ford 250 pickup truck. I could see it had been lifted and stood a lot taller than the average truck. "…I'm usually there if the trucks there, but if not, I'm probably on a beer run, just tell the guys David asked you to swing by. Let me give you my number," he said.

I passed him my phone as I had silicone on my hands and said, "Put your name in my phone, David. I would do it myself, but my hands are covered in this silicone crap." I followed up with, "I never get this much on me usually; it's because you're yakking in my ear," and chuckled as he took my phone and flipped it over.

After he gave me his number, he went to pass my phone back. I turned my body to the side and said, "slip it in my pocket, please." David slipped my phone in and said his goodbyes and headed towards his truck. It wasn't long before he had left the parking lot in his black truck. If I'm passing the area, I will give him a ring and swing in for the beer. Friendly people are hard to meet these days.

I finished my day just before three and was headed back onto the 10 freeway, following GPS to a place I had never heard of called Cactus City. As I entered the freeway and began my journey towards my location, I noticed a road sign saying, "General Patton Memorial Museum." That's near where David had said he was staying. Why not? I thought it wasn't far from my hotel location. I passed my freeway exit and followed the signs for the Patton Museum. As I pulled in and parked, I rang David to see if I needed to bring anything.

"No, Will. Nothing. We have everything here," he said. David gave me specific instructions on how to find their camp on the phone. I got back on the freeway and turned off down the next exit, Chiriaco Summit. I followed the road as David said for about two miles. I came up over the hill, and it was then I spotted David's black pickup truck. This place was in the middle of nowhere. I parked my truck behind David's and jumped out. David greeted me right away and showed me over to a motorhome, in which a man and woman sat outside on lounge chairs.

"This is Webster and Stacey," as he pointed towards the couple. "This is Will. He's from England," David said.

I said, "Hi. Nice to meet you." They both smiled

David grabbed us both a beer, and we sat in the seat facing his friends. They began talking about shooting out in the desert. I found out that David owed a Mossberg shotgun, and together they had off-loaded 250 rounds the day before. I spoke with Stacey about the UK as David and Webster carried on talking about guns and shooting.

"Do you shoot, Will?" David asked. "No, it's not my thing, David," I said with a smile back towards him.

"That's a shame, Will. Once you fire a gun, you'll love it," David smiled. I have a gun, a voice said in the back of my mind. The one I took from Jose after he tried to rob me. It was still wrapped up in a rag in my toolbox.

After talking to Stacey for a while, she mentioned she was the sister of a famous football player for San Francisco. I had never heard of him, though. She had blonde hair tied back in a ponytail, with dark brown eyes. She was about the same age as Webster, her partner, 22, or maybe, 24. She was wearing a light blue tank top and grey shorts. It was obvious she wasn't wearing a bra. I kept having to remind myself to stop looking at the outline of her nipples as they pushed her shirt out. It was undeniable; she was very good-looking.

Webster was bigger than David and looked as if he didn't fit in the seat he was sitting in. He was roughly about my height with a shaved head and a goatee type of beard. He was wearing a white t-shirt and blue denim jeans that must be roasting for him to have on in this heat.

We sat together and drank for hours. David announced he was running down to the gas station to grab some more beers. "I'll be back in twenty minutes," shouted David from the driver's seat of his truck. He drove down the hill and disappeared into the early evening darkness. The three of us sat there as we waited for David to come back. Stacey started talking to me, and as she did, Webster cut her short.

"So, you're a fucking limey then, Will?" asked Webster. His tone towards me had changed. I looked at Webster, thinking he was joking and smiled. He again asked, but louder this time, as if he thought I hadn't heard him the first time.

"So, you a fucking English limey, Will, or what?"

I responded sharply with, "Any need for the insults, Webster?" as I looked back towards him. Maybe he didn't understand the word limey wasn't a nice thing to call me.

"Is there any need for you to try chatting my girl up while I'm sitting right next to her," snarled Webster. I had no idea where Webster had gotten this idea. I was only being polite with Stacey.

"Don't be stupid, you're drunk, Webster, shut up," snapped Stacey in Webster's face.

"I think you have your wires crossed or something, mate," I responded to him. "I have a partner I'm not after another," and smiled as if to reassure him.

I could see him getting worked up as he sipped at his drink and began seriously staring right at me. "Webster, I'm not after Stacey; it's ok," I said, wishing David would return. I could see he was blind drunk.

Webster was the type of male that had yet to learn how to keep a hold of his ego and pride in check. I hoped this would calm him down, but it had the reverse effect. He became worked up very fast. I could see him becoming more agitated by the second. Just like that, he lunged towards me with his hands stretched towards my neck. The force of his weight toppled me to the ground causing me to fall backwards off my seat and onto the desert floor. We rolled back and forth until I found myself on top. Webster was big, but he was slow and cumbersome for such a big guy. I tried to calm him down, but he just kept struggling. I felt him reaching down towards my foot, so I quickly looked back, trying to avoid the hugeness of his hand coming towards me.

"KNIFE! He's going for a knife," I shouted. I saw the knife strapped to his ankle. I began to panic. I started squirming and wriggling as if my life depended on it, and at this point, I'm sure it did. I was just trying to get up off him, but he was still throwing punches towards me. I reached down as his hand pulled the knife from the sheaf; my hand grew tight around his wrist; he pulled through the strength of my left arm and set the knife towards my chest. As it neared, my right hand met my left, with both hands on his wrist. He caught the top of my ear with his left hand as I felt the punch connect. I couldn't stop both the knife and the punch. I had all my strength pushing on Webster's wrist.

I was frantic, doing everything possible to stop the tip of the blade from plunging into my chest. I moved my hips up to try and dislodge Webster's grip. I pushed forward, with a jerking moment, then again, then really hard again. I saw it in his eyes as the blade entered. At the same time, he lost his strength and grip on the knife. I continued to push and could feel every inch of the blade entering his chest. I saw the look of disbelief in his eyes. I pulled the knife out and quickly put it back in, then again and then again. I fell backwards off him and landed between his feet as he lay there, motionless.

The whole time this was occurring, I was deaf to the screams of Stacey, but now it was all I could hear. I knew I was stuck between a rock and a hard place. If I let Stacey go, she would tell the authorities what I had done. If I don't, David will be back soon, and this choice of option will no longer be available. The screaming was becoming louder in my ears. I could barely hear myself think. Suddenly, I ran towards Stacey, standing a few feet away, who was looking in shock at Webster's body. Before she had any inkling of my actions, I had hit her full force right on the side of the jaw. Her eyes snapped shut immediately, even before she hit the sand below.

I knew I only had minutes until David returned with the evening's supply of beer. I knew I had to act fast. I walked to where Webster lay. His eyes were still open, but you could see that no one remained to look back. As usual, I was numb and had no feelings about what I had just done. I just knew I did what I had to do.

Without any hesitation, I pulled the knife out of Webster's chest and ran to my truck. I opened the back, jumped inside, and grabbed the gun taken from Jose. At the same time, I dropped the knife in the back of the truck, not needing it anymore. I jumped out of the back of the truck and walked back over to where Stacey lay. I took a second to think over my next move. I could see the headlights of David's truck coming round the top of the road. I tucked the gun into my waistband and then raised both my hands as if I was signalling for him to come quick. David stopped his truck, jumped out., and came running towards me. Lucky for me, Stacey was still unconscious. I screamed, "help me get over here, start CPR. I'll call an ambulance."

"What happened?" he shouted in a tone of panic.

"We got attacked by some people," I said. He looked at me with confusion.

"Quick, start CPR." I reached into my pocket for my phone and pulled it out. I flipped the lid over, and the screen light hit my eyes, blinding me in the dark desert night. I knew I wasn't making a call but only waiting for David to start the CPR. As he placed his hands on Stacey's chest, I placed mine on the gun and pulled it out. David didn't see anything or even feel anything it happened that quick. One-shot, and it was all over. He fell flat across Stacey's body. I stood back from the scene and watched David's eyes go blank. I would like to say I enjoyed this, but David was a nice guy. A genuine person who would go out of his way to help someone. The world looks on in awe and gratitude at people like David, who never think twice about being nice. I turned to Stacey, who never came around. I shot her in the chest as she gasped for a breath, and it startled me; I pulled the trigger again out of fear, mostly.

I sat down on the tailgate of David's pickup and drank a few beers before realising I would have to clean everything up. I looked out into the night sky, searching among the stars. I looked at my phone, and it was only 7.21 pm. I knew I had to get to work —first things first, plastic sheeting and duct tape. I walked toward the truck; as I did, I noticed blood drops on my shirt. As I reached the tailgate, I said out loud, "black bags, suit, gloves." This was the basics of my first trip in the back as of the truck. I know I must be meticulous in my clean up: no evidence, nothing, not a single fingerprint. I can't even risk leaving a smudge. No footprints and eliminate as much evidence as I can. I have spent hours, days, weeks thinking about every possible scenario that could happen and how I would overcome it. When you live inside your own head as much as I do, your thinking is constant. There can be no sign that I was ever there. Anything less will mean more than my freedom. Now I knew DNA was a new thing, but I had never heard about it when all this was going on. I thought DNA was like a fingerprint.

I rolled the plastic out and cut it. One sheet per person, cut all their clothes off, place them in heavy-duty black bags, and then roll the body onto the plastic. I taped the corners of the plastic and overlapped them. I then duct-taped the three sides together to make sure nothing can get out and then rolled the body into the plastic with toughness. Duct tape all loose ends. Make a mummy out of the body. I stop after each one and had a drink, smoked a few cigarettes. I loaded the 3 of them into the back of my truck, along with the two bags of clothes I have and the knife. I headed back onto the 10 freeway.

I turned off the freeway at Rice road desert centre. This road went on for hundreds of miles with nothing, desert, rocks, mountains, and hills. The scenic route to Lake Haversu, Arizona. Home of the famous London Bridge. It was just a vast area with hardly any to no traffic—a two-lane road. I'd guess an old trucker's route, now and then you pop across a service station with a restaurant. Endless turn off roads, some go deeper still into the vast barren desert, while others climb mountain roads. Well, mountains to me. By the time I got up there, it was pitch blackout. The only light out there was from the stars in the sky. I drank a beer and smoked a few cigarettes before curling up in the back of the truck for a few hours of sleep.

I spent most of the next day digging in the desert heat. I call it the desert, as California is known for being a desert. To me, this is rocky land, more rocks and stone boulders over-sand. I had no regard at all really for Webster; I pushed his naked body into the hole with Stacey landing on top of him. I put David on the top and stood there looking at the three bodies. I somewhat wish David hadn't been there but knew none of this would have happened if he wasn't. I filled the hole back in, drinking a few cold ones along the way. I jumped back in my truck and headed for the warehouse. I was a little later pulling up at home. I ran for the shower after the day of digging in the heat of the sun. The weekend was here...

14

VICTORIA & THE SURPRISE

Parker Arizona has two banks with four ATMs. I had travelled as far East in California that you could possibly go. Now I headed across the state line to complete a few ATMs that, even though they are in Arizona, the banks were owned by the Californian department.

By the end of the first day, I was drained from the heat. California is hot but usually had a sea breeze. While Arizona was just plain hot without any kind of breeze or cool relief whatsoever. It was easily 112 degrees most days. As I parked the truck outside the hotel, my body craved a cold beer and a bite to eat.

I have a quick shower, changed into some shorts, and set out to find a place to eat. I passed a Denny's at the first intersection, but I saw a Golden Burger restaurant in the distance. I carried on walking because breakfast at Denny's wouldn't work for me right now.

As I cut across the parking lot, my phone started to ring; it was Madison. We tended to speak to one another most days. Madison and I had been seeing each other off and on for a while now. The relationship was good, but neither of us wanted anything full-on. Madison was just checking how my day had been and making sure I would still call into hers on my way back home after work on Thursday.

We finished talking, and I put my last cigarette out and headed into the burger joint. The place was quiet; I was the only customer in there. I was greeted by a Hispanic man, who leaned out the window from the kitchen area and told me someone would be with me shortly to take my order. The place wasn't very big; it comprised a kitchen, a counter, and five tables with benches around them. I sat at a table in the corner, looking out as the busy traffic rushing by on the intersection.

A young Hispanic-looking lady then greeted me. She was only young, in her early twenties, I would guess. She was dressed all in white: white shorts, a white polo shirt and bright white sneakers. It was her waitress uniform. She had short black hair, dark brown eyes, and was very small, barely five feet. I ordered my usual drink, a Coors and then did the usual English thing again, back, and forth for several minutes. My waitress was called Victoria. She was besotted with my accent, so much so, she wouldn't leave me alone. I didn't mind; to be honest, it was a huge ego boost. Victoria sat with me, chatting while I ate my burger and fries. We talked about England, California, and what I had been up to over the last few years. Victoria explained how she ended up working in Golden Burgers a year back, but nothing better had come up, so she had stayed here.

As I was finishing up my burger, Victoria began talking, "So what you doing tonight then, Will?" she asked.

"Nothing, Victoria. I'm going to grab a few beers and head back to my hotel room. What are you doing?" I asked back.

She smiled and responded, "I'm working sadly. Here is my phone number, Will. I'm off after tonight until the weekend. If you want to grab a drink one night?" and smiled at me.

I gave Victoria a small hug and let her know I would call her tomorrow after work and then left. I grabbed a six-pack from the 7-11 and went back to my hotel room for the night. I texted back and forth with Cameron and Madison most of the evening while replying to work emails on my laptop.

The next day was hotter than the first, reaching 117 degrees. I was melting in the heat. Once I had finished work, I drove the truck into the hotel's parking lot and tried to ring Victoria. I didn't get an answer, but she called me back minutes later. "Sorry, Will. I was in the hot tub and couldn't reach my phone. What are you doing tonight?"

"I don't have any plans yet, Victoria," I replied.

"Do you want to come back to mine, Will? We can drink a few beers in the hot tub together?"

I smiled before replying. "Why not Victoria." I arranged to meet her by the 7-11 near the restaurant to walk over to her place from there.

I walked up and met Victoria, who was wearing a light blue t-shirt, a pair of black leggings, and a pair of sandals. I looked at her arse in the nylon of the leggings and thought, oh my. It was then I knew in my head how the night was going to play out. I grabbed a twelve-pack of beers and some cigarettes from the 7-11 before we walked over to Victoria's place. It wasn't more than a few minutes walk.

We walked around a few corners as I tried to focus, so I knew my way back. Once we got to Victoria's, we sat out back together on a couple-style lounge chair with two cold beers in our hands. "Did you bring a swimming costume?" Victoria said as she started undressing. Victoria started to remove all her clothes with no shame, dropping each item in front of me until she was completely naked. I looked at her perfectly shaped, tanned body and thought, how perky her breasts looked.

"No, I didn't think of that," and smiled back. Victoria's naked body climbed into the hot tub.

"That's okay," she said. "It will be more fun watching you undress." She rested her head on her arm and got into a comfy position to watch me. I stripped my clothes off and made an awkward attempt to do a small striptease for Victoria. If nothing else, I was amusing her. Poor Victoria had no idea of the type of man she had invited into her home. I pulled my boxers down to expose myself. I climbed into the hot tub and sat opposite Victoria. Once I was sat down, I could feel her foot rubbing my manhood. I could feel myself waking up. I must stop her. I knew this wasn't about sex. I can have sex anytime I want; this was something more, a primal need that lurked deep within my soul. I thought of Madison on all fours, with me standing behind her. Poor Victoria had no idea what was about to happen.

I reached my hands into the water and grasped both her ankles in my hands. In one quick motion, I pulled her legs towards me, which pulled her off the step she had been sitting on, causing her head to go underwater. I stood up fast and pulled her ankles up out of the water, so her top section was still left in the water. I pushed my weight down on top of her legs just as she began to struggle.

"You might as well just give in," I said out loud. Although I'm sure with her head under the water, she didn't hear me. Victoria struggled for a little before going limp. I let her feet go, and they dropped into the water. Her head popped up out of the water. Her eyes were open and staring blankly towards me. I sat on the edge of the hot tub and drank my beer. Victoria had no idea what was happening, and by the time she realised, it was already too late.

I finished my beer and watched Victoria's body float across the water. When I had finished, I got out and dried myself with the towels Victoria had put on the back door and then put my clothes back on. I went into the kitchen area; under the sink, I found my old friends, the black bags. Using the wet towel, I wiped the handles that I had touched and then returned to the back area. I bagged up Victoria's clothes and my empty beer bottles. I used the towel to wipe the case of beers down we had just bought before placing it in the black bag. I tied the black bag closed. I have got to exit and do it quickly and quietly so as not to be noticed. I tucked the bag under my arm and went through the door. The street was empty; I couldn't see anybody around. I made haste quickly up the street and made it back towards the 7-11 near the burger joint. I knew I was safe.

I went back to the hotel and spent the rest of the evening chatting with Madison, Joe, and Cameron on my phone.

For the following two days, I kept a low profile. I didn't go out after work and just had a few beers back in the hotel room each night. On Thursday, I finished early and was happy to be heading towards Madison's place. One night with Madison, then the warehouse in the morning, before I could start my weekend. As I left the freeway and entered Beaumont, I was relieved the workweek was over.

I pulled the truck up outside Madison's house and went in the front door. "Hi babe," she shouted as I walked into the hall. She came rushing around the corner and hugged me tightly. I hugged her back, and the aroma of her body rubbed onto mine.

"Can we go out for food, please, Will? I'm not in the mood to cook tonight," Madison asked.

"That works for me, Hun. Any ideas what we can have?"

"I know a quiet place on the outskirts of Banning. We can sit and talk there. Get ready. I'm starving," she announced.

I dropped my bag onto the floor and said loudly, "I'm ready.". Madison drove, which was strange, as we would usually get a taxi. She said it wasn't close, and she didn't mind driving so I could have a drink.

We got to the restaurant and were seated at a table beneath the window. There wasn't much to look at, just open mountains and flat desert land all around. I listened as Madison told me about her workday. She announced that her mother was wondering if we could all go for dinner together one night. I had been seeing Madison casually now for a few years but never met her parents. There wasn't any need; I knew Madison was happy with our casual relationship. We sat and ate; the restaurant was becoming busier as the evening went on. We didn't mind; we became lost in our bubble. We finished our food and headed towards Madison's car. As I gripped the handle, she grabbed me by my arm and turned me around. "Will," she stopped. "Will, I need to tell you something." I looked at Madison, who had a worried look on her face.

"What's up, Hun?" I said, with curiosity in my eyes.

"I'm late," she said.

"Late for what?" I responded and checked my watch.

"No, no, Will. I'm late as in my period never came."

"Oh," I said in a shocked tone.

"I'm pregnant, Will. I have done three different home kits, and they all came back positive. I went to visit my doctor yesterday, who also confirmed I'm pregnant." She stood looking into my eyes as if trying to read my thoughts.

"OH MY." I looked at her in disbelief.

"It's yours, Will. What do you think?" as she looked at me again. My mind began working fast. I knew this would happen eventually. I had the sudden image of being a Daddy, running about after a little one. I wonder if it's a boy or girl? What will it be called? My mind cascaded down the list until I got to the happy parts and smiled towards Madison.

"I'm going to be a Daddy. IM GOING TO BE A DADDY," I shouted in the parking lot.

"Ssssshhhh, Will," Madison said. "Don't tell everyone." I grabbed Madison with both hands and pulled her into an embrace.

"Are you okay with this, Madison?" I asked and released her a little from my hug.

"Yes, Will. I'm pleased about it. I wasn't sure how you would react. Are you okay with this, Will?" she asked and looked me right in the eyes.

"I'm over the moon about it, Madison. I'm going to be a Daddy." We hugged in the parking lot and sat and talked for nearly an hour. We shared our thoughts about the two of us becoming parents and how we intended to do everything right with this child. I knew it wasn't going to end up with the local authority, that's for sure. I was determined to make an awesome dad.

As we exited the freeway and headed back to Beaumont, I asked Madison to stop at the bar so we could have a quick drink. Mostly to steady my nerves, I was on edge, excited and scared, all in the same moment.

As we parked up and got out, Madison pulled me back by my shirt. "Will, please, don't say anything about being pregnant in the bar. Beaumont is a small place, and gossip travels fast. I need to tell my parents before we tell everyone else."

"Oh, of course, Madison. I won't say a word in here." As we went to walk in, I pulled the door open for Madison to enter. Before the door closed, I looked across the parking lot and saw the black Chevy Blazer with the yellow snake decal on the back window. It was parked up not too far away. I thought whoever is parking in my spot outside Madison's is in here now. I mentioned it to Madison, who laughed it off, as we entered the bar.

The place was busy when we went got inside. I grabbed a beer for myself, and Madison had an orange juice. We sat out in the poolroom, and Madison played pool with some friends she knew from school. I just sat back and enjoyed the moment. I'm going to be a dad, I thought excitingly. I went to the restroom and then went back to the bar to grab another drink. As I walked back out, I could see Madison talking to some younger guy with her back to me. He was in his early twenties, about my height but slightly bigger in body mass than me. He was wearing blue jean shorts, a white tank top and was covered in tattoos up both his arms. He had spiky blond hair and blue eyes. As I got near them, the guy looked over Madison's shoulder to see me approaching and smiled, whispered something to Madison, and then walked off.

"You, okay?" I asked Madison and stepped to her side.

"Yeah, I'm fine. Just some guy I know from work is all. Are you playing?" she said and waved a pool cue towards me.

"Yeah, okay. I'm shit, though," and we both laughed.

We played a few games of pool. Madison won most of them, but it was fun watching her bend and spread across the table. I took the opportunity to grope her as much as possible. Once we finished our drinks, we decided to go.

We went back to Madison's and sat in the kitchen until late at night, talking about becoming parents. We found out both of us have very different ideas of being parents. But we agreed to disagree on a few things because we knew this would be fun, however, also a learning period. The following morning, I didn't rush out the door like I would most Fridays. I stayed and had breakfast with Madison and told her that I would call her over the weekend.

The drive back to the warehouse seemed longer than usual. My mind was all over the place; I will have to tell Joe, Tess, and Cameron. They had heard about Madison but never met her. As far as Joe and Cameron knew, Madison was just a booty call. This was true at the time, but things had changed. I unloaded the truck at the warehouse and loaded it up for the next week. I knew the truck would be parked outside Joe's all weekend.

When I got home, the house was packed. This was just normal now; Tess was living there, and Cameron was as well. There wasn't a day gone by when one or a few of their friends wouldn't just show up. As I walked out back, I could see Tess and Cameron lying at the side of the pool. Jess and Kristen were all in the pool, playing about with one another. I grabbed a beer and took off my shirt. Cameron came and sat next to me to hear about how my week had been. I was dying to tell her about Madison. Cameron will make the perfect aunt, and Joe will be an amazing uncle. I knew not to say anything until I had both Joe and Cameron together alone.

Before long, I was in my shorts and fooling about in the pool with Jess. Joe showed up a little after five. We ordered a takeout that night and ate it all cramped together around the patio table. As we had nearly finished, Joe began to talk.

"Now that I have my besties here together. I want to talk to you both," as he looked at myself and Cameron. We all looked at Joe, waiting for him to continue. "Will, Cam, I have some news for you. I asked Tess to marry me a few weeks back, and she has said yes."

"Oh, my lord," Cameron said as she jumped up and rushed to hug Joe and Tess.

"Congratulations, guys," I said and smiled broadly.

"Will you be my best man, Will?" Joe asked me excitingly.

"Of course, I will, Joe," as I pulled him out of his seat to hug him.

"Next June, well, the 4th to be exact. I have arranged a priest to marry us down on the beach." He smiled towards Tess. I could see how happy the two of them were together. Cameron looked at me and smiled. I knew, like myself, that she was really happy for Joe. Since she moved in, Tess had become like a sister to us, and she and Joe were made for one another. Tess was a grounding rod for Joe, and he needed that in his life; and in Tess, he found someone he could love the way he wanted and be himself at the same time.

We all went out on Saturday night to celebrate. I was left with Jess and Kristen most of the night because Joe and Tess were dancing together. Cameron and Roland argued all night long. Roland left early, which annoyed Cameron, as she considered this "running away from an argument, " so she went after him. Joe and Tess were ready to go by midnight.

We got a cab back to the house, and as Joe and Tess headed for the bedroom, I grabbed a beer and sat out on the patio. Wow, what a week! From Victoria to finding out I'm going to become a dad, to becoming a best man, I'm going to have to sit down with Joe and Cameron and explain about Madison and the baby. What the fuck am I going to do as a dad? I was lost in my thoughts when Joe came running out onto the patio. "He's done it again" he says, angry. I can see Joe is upset.

"What's going on, Joe?" I snapped right back.

"He's hit her again. I'm going to fucking kill him this time," he screamed back at me.

"Where is she, Joe?" I demanded, jumping from my seat.

"She is in a cab coming back here; she's in tears, Will. If he's hurt her, I'm going to hurt him," he said with rage in his eyes.

Tess came out back only seconds before Cameron showed up. Cameron looked shaken when she came in, her top lip looked all fat and swollen, and her wrists had bruises on them as if he had restrained her arms. We grabbed her the second she got in the back. She immediately started sobbing and broke down in our arms.

"He punched me in the mouth for nothing and called me a whore. I thought he had left, but he came back again and threw me up against the wall and held me while he spat in my face."

Joe shouted, "HE'S DEAD!" We sat there for a few hours, and between Tess and me, we managed to calm Joe down.

We drank a few more beers, and I said, "I'm heading off to bed, guys. I'm done in." Everybody said goodnight as I walked towards the patio doors. Right before, I stopped and turned around, addressing all three of them, said, "You all know that Madison and I have been seeing each other off and on. Well, she's pregnant. I'll be bringing her home next weekend to meet you all."

"What?!" shrieked Cameron as they all rushed and grabbed me.

"Congratulations, Will", said Joe as he hugged me tightly. I

walked off to bed, smiling to myself. I lay on top of the sheets and messaged Madison to tell her I have told them. I knew she wouldn't be awake, but that didn't stop me. I was slowly slipping away when I heard a knock on the door. It was Joe. "Hey Will, I'm going to kill that guy. Who the fuck does he think he is touching Cameron?"

"Joe, it's late right now. Let's think about this before we make any decisions that could be done in haste," I said. He agreed with me, and we decided to do nothing until next weekend. He wished me congratulations again and then closed the door. I lay there wide awake at first, thinking about Roland and how he had been warned.

15

ETHAN

The following week dragged in work. I knew I was nervous about Joe, Tess, and Cameron meeting Madison at the weekend. It was very important to me they all got on. I planned to pick Madison up, go to the warehouse to unload, and head home. This nearly went according to plan, but I had to sit around for nearly an hour while Madison packed her bags. I didn't mind. I had sat waiting on Cameron to get ready so many times before that I had become used to waiting on women.

Joe, Tess, and Cameron were already home when I pulled the truck in and parked it to the side. All their cars had been parked in a line to leave me space for the truck. "Give me a second," I said to Madison, jumping out and run around the front of the truck to help her down. I could see in Madison's eyes that she was anxious. "It's ok, babe, you will get on great with them. Don't fret," I said with a smile. I could see Madison felt at ease a little after this. I grabbed our bags and headed inside.

I showed Madison in first and then dropped the bags by the couch in the living room. "The guys will all be on the patio; let us grab a drink and join them." I smiled at Madison and walked into the kitchen and grabbed a handful of beers. "This way, babe," I said as I gestured onto the patio. As we walked out, I yelled,

"Honey, I'm home," and laughed loudly to myself. I was greeted immediately by Joe, who reached towards me and grabbed some of the bottles I had brought out.

"Let me give you a hand," he said, putting the remainder of the beers on the table. Cameron hugged me gently and gave me a peck on the cheek. I could feel the wetness of her bikini covering the shirt I was wearing. I smiled toward Tess, who was sitting behind the table. I reached in and gave her a quick kiss on the cheek. All three of them were dressed in swimwear. Cameron had her light blue bikini on, and I knew this was her favourite bikini because she had told me how hard it was to find one that fitted correctly. Tess had on a black and white bikini. Joe was wearing his Bermuda shorts that he loved so much.

"This is Madison, guys," as I looked towards all three of them. "Madison, this is Tess, Joe, and Cameron," pointing at each in turn. I could see Madison was a little standoffish until Joe grabbed hold of her and gave her a huge hug. Both the girls followed suit.

"I didn't pack a bikini," Madison said as she looked at me.

Cameron jumped right in with, "Don't you worry, babe. I've got loads, and so has Tess," Tess smiled back. I pulled a seat out for Madison and passed her a drink and sat myself down at the table. We all sat drinking and talking. I spoke to Joe when he asked me questions or spoke to me, but I was more into listening today. I wanted to see how they all acted towards Madison. I know Joe and Cameron very well but was still figuring Tess out. If I like her, I'm sure they will also. They all sat and talked between themselves. Cameron and Madison had already hit it off. It's hard for Cameron not to like someone automatically. It's just the way she behaved. Before long, the girls had got Madison a bikini, and the three of them were in the pool, laughing and fooling around. Joe had come and sat down next to me at the table as we watched the girls in the pool.

"Did you figure out what to do with Roland?" Joe asked me. I had hardly said two words to him since I got home, as Madison was getting to know everyone.

"Straight to the point, Joe?" I asked inquisitively but still half laughing.

"Sorry, Will. It's been in my head all week. He's been calling and texting Cam non-stop. Some texts are saying how sorry he is and the next calling her a whore or slut. He needs to be stopped."

"Ok, Joe. I'm with you on this. It's just I have brought Madison here to meet you all. Let's talk about this when we get home from the club. Madison is excited to see a club in LA because it had been a few years since she has been to Los Angeles," I said and looked at him in a way to ask him to let it go for now. Joe took the hint and didn't push the Roland issue anymore. I knew something had to be done to stop him. I just hadn't had time to think about everything going on.

That evening we all got ready to go out that night. As we waited for Joe and Cameron to come out of their rooms, Tess and Madison began playing with each other's hair. "My wallet," I said as I realised, I had left it in my room. I entered my room and looked for my wallet. Once I had it in my hand and put it in the back pocket of my trousers, Cameron stepped into my room.

"Roland is calling my phone constantly. I think I'm going to change my number," she said immediately.

I laughed loudly and sharply responded, "What, you think that's going to stop him bothering you?"

"I don't know how else to make him stop calling me," she replied.

"Let's not worry about it tonight, Cam," I said. "WE ARE GOING OUT," I shouted excitingly, in a futile attempt to stop her thinking about Roland again. It looked like it had worked, but for how long, I'm unsure.

We left home as soon as the town car that Cameron had booked for us arrived. We all jumped in the back. I could see Madison was excited to be going to STARZ. I talked about the place near enough every time I saw her. We did a quick stop at the shop to grab cigarettes and then set off for STARZ. We loved this nightclub; it was ours, and we didn't even pay to go in anymore.

We knew all the staff and the majority of the customers as well. Tonight, looked as if it was going well. The fact that all the people I loved liked Madison made it all the better.

The nightclub was packed, but it always was after ten, even on weeknights. It was nice to watch and enjoy the company. I was with Madison and Tess, dancing with the two of them most of the night. Jess and Kristen showed up not long after us. I think both were already drunk when they got here. We all had a really good night. Well, except Cameron, who was constantly watching the doorway or looking around all evening. It was clear how nervous she was to be there. Roland wouldn't be stupid enough to show up here. I think I was the only one to notice Cameron wasn't herself. I was becoming irritated inside. I could feel myself becoming enraged. I tried to calm myself as I leaned into Joe, who was next to me and said, "Be up for six in the morning and meet me in the garage; you're driving." I looked at him. I knew he heard what I had said, but I needed to see he understood.

It took only a second before Joe smiled and said, "Thanks, Will." We left STARZ not long after two, but by the time we got home, it was nearly three in the morning. I knew I wouldn't sleep tonight. We all sat out the back on the patio drinking. I watched as Joe sipped a beer for over an hour. He knew I was serious about leaving at six. Tess and Madison headed off to bed first, and Cameron wasn't far behind them. Joe and I sat alone on the patio.

"What time do you have, Joe?" I asked.

"Just gone ten past four, Will," Joe responded as he looked up from his watch.

"Let's go now, Joe, and hopefully, none of the women will wake up when we're gone," I whispered. Joe stood up and smiled, pulling the car keys from his pocket.

"I'm ready, Will," he responded. I knew he would be ready as soon as I told him in the club. We quietly entered the garage, and as Joe climbed in the driver's seat, I grabbed a hammer sitting on the workbench and climbed into the car. I put the hammer down to my side and fastened my seatbelt. I could see the look on Joe's face when he realised what we were about to do to Roland. I'll never forget it. "Dead, Will. So, we are going to kill him? I thought we would just beat him up."

"Sorry, Joe. It's gone past that point now. I hate seeing Cameron scared, even more so when there is something I can do to stop it." Once we got the car out the gate and down Canyon Drive, I explained to Joe what would happen. I told him that all I needed him to do was drive and stay in the car. Joe argued with me for a few minutes until I got the point across. I didn't need him, and it would be safer for me to do this alone.

I had Joe park a street away from Roland's on purpose, not wanting to be heard or seen by anyone coming. As I neared his house, I could see how dark it was. I looked around at the surrounding houses to see if I could see anyone. The street was quiet. I walked to his front door and looked quietly through the letterbox. All the lights were off, so I rang the doorbell a few times and waited. I looked around the street. I couldn't see any lights on in the surrounding houses. I waited, but nothing happened. He wasn't home. Perhaps, he was out clubbing. I rang the doorbell repeatedly and was just about to leave when a light went on in the hall. He's home, I thought. I pulled my shirt up and got the hammer ready. I looked down at my hand as it gripped the handle of the hammer. The door opened, and as it started to open, I pushed it hard and fast with all my might. This forced the door wide open, and it crashed loudly against the entrance wall.

As it sprung to its end, Roland was in front of me, looking shocked. I raised the hammer and brought it down on his head. As it connected, I could see he had just woken up. He must have been sleeping. I brought the hammer down again, then again, and again, each blow perfectly timed to strike his head. After about four to five swings of the hammer, he was out, lying in a heap on the floor. I dragged his body to the wall and sat him up against it. I pushed the front door slightly but not fully closed with my foot. No, I wasn't finished with Roland. I had come this far and wasn't stopping now. I slapped him a couple of times to wake him up. I made him open his eyes and listen to me. He was disorientated. I told him how close Cameron was to me, how much she means to me, how she even married me to make me a legal citizen in America. I told him then about Daryl and the damage a baseball bat can do. Roland's bloodied face looked scared. I told him how easy it was to make a body disappear in the blink of an eye.

"Please, please, Will," he began pleading. I was done with listening. I had heard these pleas before from Jose. I started swinging the hammer freely. I stopped counting. I wasn't even bothered, as his blood splashed all over my face and body. I just kept on swinging until all that remained was unrecognisable. I'm glad this guy met me. I knew the last thing he would see was my face.

"You won't be touching Cameron ever again," I snarled towards his bloody corpse. I tucked the bloody hammer under my arm and stood up. I looked over at Roland and watched as the pile of blood he was sitting in began to spread. The blood was everywhere; it had splattered up the walls and across the ceiling. I was covered in blood.

"Get going, Will", a voice shouted into my mind. I used my t-shirt to close the door by the handle. I looked around at the houses to see if the sounds had waked anyone. Nothing had changed; all the lights were still off. I set about my escape. I ran this time as fast as I could until I reached the end of the road. I slowed down to a fast walk and turned onto a side street, which was very quiet, and then onto the street, Joe was parked. I got back to the car and climbed into the passenger seat.

"Fuck, Will. Are you ok?" Joe looked at me, worried, "you're covered in blood."

"Don't worry, Joe, it's not mine. Let's go, please. I don't want to be here any longer than I need to be. Drive safe, please Joe, we can't afford to get pulled over with me looking like this," as I laughed. Joe drove us back home. I explained how Roland didn't see it even coming and how I beat him with the hammer to Joe as he drove. I didn't go into details; I didn't tell him what I said to him or even how his head looked as I left. It was slowly becoming light as we pulled through the gate at home.

I stripped my clothes off in the garage. Joe put each article into a black bag along with the bloody hammer. Once Joe checked the coast was clear, I headed into the shower. Joe followed me and began washing his hands in the sink. "I'm going to bed, Will. See you in the morning," as he squeezed my shoulder and left the bathroom.

I looked in the mirror at myself; I was covered in Roland's blood; it was across my face, all over my head, up to my arms, right down my legs, from head to toe. I stepped in the shower and watched the red water swirl at my feet. I began having thoughts about Madison and then the baby. I had images of me behind bars, and the realisation of never seeing my child or watching them grow up hit home. If I carry on with this lifestyle, I will end up dead or in prison for the rest of my life. I thought about the fun that I would have with my child. I don't care if it's a boy or a girl; it will be mine either way. I thought about José next, who had tried to rob me and then through everyone right back to Daryl. I've killed thirteen people now, but it was only after Daryl that I started to enjoy murder. I liked how my heart pounded, the fear of being caught, and the adrenaline. I loved the feeling of killing, having the power to end a life, as easy as clicking my fingers. This was all before I knew Madison was carrying my child. If I want to see how my child will grow up, I can't carry on killing people for my enjoyment. I'm going to have to stop. Can I stop? I must try. I began thinking about the alternative. I must choose my baby or my killing spree? It must be the baby. I could have stood in the shower the rest of the night, but I forced myself out.

As I walked across the living room, I looked to see the sun was already high above the skyline of Los Angeles. I climbed into bed with Madison, who gave a cute little groan as I snuggled into her. I kissed the back of her neck and put my hand on her stomach. I drifted into sleep thinking about becoming a dad and how happy this thought made me feel inside.

As my eyes opened the following morning, I realised I was alone in bed. I looked at my alarm clock on the nightstand, which read 3.12 in the afternoon. It was quite clearly no longer the morning because I had slept most of the day. I got up and threw my shorts on and walked through the living room. Cameron was coming in the patio doors. "Morning, babe. Coffee or beer?" as she walked into the kitchen.

"Coffee, please, Cam. I need to wake up first," as I walked onto the patio. She brought my coffee out. Madison, who was in the pool with Joe and Tess, jumped out to give me a morning kiss.

"What time did you come to bed?" she asked.

"It was late. It's his fault," I said with a smile on my face, pointing towards Joe in the pool swimming. "He kept me awake all night drinking." Joe just smiled at me. I decided not to go out that night as I was too tired. Before I knew what was going on, Cameron and Tess were on their phones.

"Ok, we'll have people around tonight instead then," said Cameron. The house wasn't packed that night, but there were a few people who came over. Mostly just friends of Cameron's and Tess's that we already knew.

On Sunday, just after lunch, we hit the road. I dropped Madison back at her house in Beaumont and headed off to my next hotel. I was happy about how the weekend had gone.

On Monday, I sat down to eat lunch, and then Joe called me to let me know that two detectives had shown up that morning and told Cameron that Roland was dead. They had also asked about her whereabouts on Friday / early Saturday morning. Joe said they left after he and Tess had told them she was with them all night. He said how shocked Cameron was to hear the news; the detective thinks it might have been a robbery gone wrong. I asked him if Cam was "ok", and Joe responded, "she will be now, thanks to us. Well, it was all you, Will."

"It was us, Joe. I couldn't have done it without you."

A couple of weeks later, Cameron, Joe, and Tess filled out a statement with the detectives, and that was the last time we heard from them. Roland's case would become a cold case without any further evidence. I began to let the image of Roland's face slip from my mind.

Over the next few months, as Madison became bigger, we began connecting more than we ever had. I could feel myself starting to fall in love with her. It wasn't hard to do, but it felt a little strange going from casual sex buddies to being full-time partners. Madison was easy to get on with, really; it was me who needed to adjust. I was doing this because I was excited to become a daddy. Each weekend we would drive up to LA until it started becoming too much for Madison, so we started spending our weekends in Beaumont. I had to go back to Los Angeles every Friday to the warehouse, so I would stay at home on Friday and be back to Madison's for the rest of the weekend. Overall, life was going well. When the baby did arrive, it was a bouncing baby boy. We called him Ethan because this was the only name we could agree on after a week of heated debate. I was happy. I mean, really happy. For the first time in my life, I had someone to love unconditionally. I would never have imagined all those years ago, sat in the cosy corner café, that I would end up here.

16

THE WEDDING

Come the following March, and it was all go for Joe and Tess. The wedding was less than a month away. I stayed there when I was in Los Angles on Friday, but this routine was solely coming to an end now. My new position had started, and I was flying in and out of Arizona all the time. In the beginning, I had a few rocky starts that cost Wincapa a few $5000 fines for not being "Live" on time. However, Bernard helped me figure out what I was doing wrong, and everything began running smoothly in time. Before long, the job became much easier. I managed to find contractors all over Arizona to do the work. I was shocked to see the estimates from contractor forms, ranging from $22 to $36 thousand per ATM. I now see why Bernard hired me because it worked out a lot cheaper for the company overall.

Ethan was my joy. I couldn't wait to see him every weekend. He was nearly six months old and growing so faster I couldn't keep up. I spent all my time thinking about him. He was my whole world, my everything, a part of me I never knew existed.

Between my friends in Los Angeles and Madison's parents, Ethan was spoilt rotten. I had, of course, met Madison's parents by that time. Every time I came home, I found them there each week. Ethan was their only grandchild. Madison's mother, Janna, was very controlling at first, but I nicely put her straight so as to keep the harmony. Madison's dad, Kevin, was like me. Every time he saw Ethan, he turned to mush. This was funny to witness, because he was a huge, burly trucker, after all.

When the wedding date came around in April, we had a custom made suit done for Ethan, so he looked like one of the lads; he looked super cute.

The wedding was amazing. Joe had arranged to get married on the beach. Considering it was just family and close friends, there were still close to two hundred people at the ceremony. Joe had arranged for private cars to take us to and from the beach. Being the best man, I was glued to Joe from the evening before. Tess and Cameron had gone to stay at Tess' apartment in Hollywood. He was nervous at the thought of marriage, but he knew he loved Tess. When it came to the "I do" parts, Cameron started crying. This set Ethan off, who was sitting next to her on Madison's lap. It was funny to watch how the priest became louder to muffle out Ethan's cries.

When the ceremony was over, we all headed off to the reception. I had to do a best man's speech, the first and only one I've ever done. I hadn't embarrassed Joe too much. I told the room how I've never met a more sincere, honest, and trustworthy friend. I said how Tess came into his life, and that was when he changed and became even happier. By the time I had met all the families, I was completely drained. We all left the reception around five and headed home. The house was heaving with people. Most were just family members making sure everything was alright and if they needed anything. In the evening, we had a huge outdoor party that Joe and Tess had arranged. It was like our own personal nightclub.

Joe and Tess honeymooned in Barbados for a month. Why not? I thought when Joe had told me this plan a few weeks earlier as we sat on our patio

Once they came home, we all just fell into our routines and carried on living life.

I had had a tough week in flagstaff; one day, the contractors didn't even show up. This would happen from time to time. Small contractors would often pull out at the last minute. I couldn't wait to get home and see Ethan and Madison on Friday morning. I was up and out of Los Angeles by five am. It was just after eight am when I pulled up in the driveway. The sun was already shining in the morning sky. Madison's car was in the driveway. I let myself in quietly so as not to wake anyone. I knew Ethan had been keeping Madison up all week, and she had trouble putting him down each night. The house was dark and quiet. I crept down the hall to the bedroom. The door was slightly ajar; I looked in and could see Madison lying naked on top of the bed. A guy was lying naked next to her.

"What?" I whispered under my breath. I became lightheaded, almost as if I had just bounced off a train going at top speed. My stomach dropped. I had a feeling like my heart had stopped for a second or two. I stepped back into the hall in shock. I crouched down with my back along the wall and put my head in my hands. Why? Why would she do this to me? I love her. She can't love me? Surely not? I was devastated. I had never had this feeling in me before. It was like my heart was breaking into pieces in my chest. Then it started: the rage. I could feel myself becoming angry. I was on the verge of breaking down the door.

In a few seconds flat, I was standing in the kitchen with a cleaver in my hands. I will fucking kill them both. I started out of the kitchen and heading towards the hall. I had beaten Roland with a hammer, so he was unrecognisable for touching Cameron. I'm going to fucking mutilate this guy.

As I travelled down the hallway, I heard Ethan crying. This was as if a light switch had been flicked on inside my mind. I instantly became calm. I could hear Madison moving around in the bedroom. The rage was dissolving in my stomach quicker than it came. I was no longer shaking with anger. I couldn't leave him without a mother. However, a big part of me wanted her dead also.

I walked quietly back to the kitchen and put the knives back in the drawer. I walked over and sat on the couch, and rested my head in my hands. I felt utterly lost. Why would Madison do this to me? And Ethan, of course. Did she ever really love me?

A few seconds later, Madison entered the room, carrying Ethan. I took my head out of my hands. As soon as she saw me, she stopped in her tracks. "Hey babe, when did you get home?" she said as she walked towards the kettle and switched it on. She turned and walked towards me, attempting to pass Ethan to me and said, "can you hold him while I run to the toilet." I looked at Madison, and from the look alone, she knew it was too late. "I'm sorry, Will. I really am; please forgive me, please." I raised my hand as if to say stop, enough.

"Stop talking." She went quiet. "Why, that's all I want to know, just why?"

Not listening to me, she returned to saying, "Please, Will. I'm sorry. I didn't know what I was doing. Please forgive me, Will," as she took a step towards me in an attempt to try and hold me.

"NO MADISON," I snarled towards her in anger.

"Please, Will. Can I tell you what happened?"

I laughed loudly as I stood up. "No, thanks, you're ok, Madison. Get that man out of the bed so I can pack."

"Will, please."

"NOW MADISON or I'm no longer responsible for what I do to you and him," I growled with rage.

Madison placed Ethan in his playpen and rushed out of the room. I sat and looked at my son one last time. My heart was breaking. Ethan was oblivious to anything going on around him. This, however, didn't stop me from feeling for him. This poor kid, I thought, sitting there. I heard the noises of the guy rushing about as Madison came in and stood by the kitchen doorway.

"He's parked in the garage, and your car is parked in the driveway," she half-whispered, as though she had become ashamed of herself.

I stood up, walked out, and got in my car. I had to take a

breath or two before starting it up. I reversed back off the driveway as the garage door opened. It was then I saw it—a black Chevy Blazer with a yellow snake decal on the window. My heart sank deeper in my chest. As the Chevy pulled past me, I looked at the guy and recognised him. He had been talking to Madison that night in the bar. It was the guy, she said, "she knew from work." He didn't even glance in my direction as he drove away. Had she been seeing him all this time? Have I been played as a fool for these past two years? I was becoming angry again. I pulled back in the driveway as the Chevy Blazer sped out of the street. I was packed in minutes flat; anything I didn't pack, I didn't need. Madison tried stopping me from leaving a few more times and even tried holding onto me and blocking the exit to the door. I hugged and kissed Ethan and left. I got in the car and drove off. Before I turned the corner, I looked in my rear-view mirror. I could see Madison was standing in the driveway. I jumped onto the freeway.

I drove faster than I have ever driven for the first twenty miles, heading back to Los Angeles. It was only when I noticed a cop car going the other way on the freeway did I slow down. I made it back home. Well, Joe's house. I called Madison's home now. This was my home, still either way. Before he had got married, Joe told Cameron and me that this was always going to be our home. I walked in and could hear the girls in the back. I put my bags in my room, looked in the mirror to compose myself, and then headed out the back.

"Good afternoon," I said as I walked out. There was nothing about the afternoon that had been good for me, I thought.

"You're back; that was quick," said Cameron with a smile. I sat in my seat, and she passed me a beer. I told Tess and Cameron what had happened, and they were as shocked as me.

"Why would she do that, Will?" asked Tess, with a look of confusion on her face.

I shrugged my shoulders. I couldn't understand it. Ethan was what had brought us together. I was already missing him. Within the next hour, Joe was home; both Tess and Cameron had texted him to let him know what happened.

"No fucking way, bud," said Joe as he walked up to me and grabbed me in a hug.

"I left Ethan there, Joe," I said, as I could feel myself becoming emotional.

"It's ok, Will. Don't worry, you will see him again."

I didn't see Ethan the next day, but Madison did show up. Crying, saying how she had made a huge mistake and wished it had never happened. Madison begged me, sobbing and screaming, for us to give it another go. I knew as I sat on the couch the morning before in her kitchen that this was over. Madison just hadn't realised how lucky she was. And yet again, Ethan saved a few more lives. As I would no longer be in the same room as Madison, she refused to allow me to see Ethan. I had to start a court case to see my son.

During the case, I was given the option to have a court-appointed DNA test. I had to provide a DNA sample to the courts to prove I was the father. I wasn't going to do it, but both Tess and Cameron insisted that I did. Thirty days later, I got a phone call from my attorney. The DNA test came back as negative for me being the father. I had the feeling my legs had been kicked out from under me. Whatever was left of my heart broke into a thousand pieces. I hurt more than I had ever hurt in my entire life. Ethan had become my whole life, my baby boy. I began crying, then snarled as I became enraged.

"I SHOULD HAVE FUCKING KILLED THEM BOTH," I screamed at the top of my voice.

Cameron rushed out to the patio and hugged me tightly. I knew I couldn't change anything, but I missed my little man, Ethan. I think about him all the time. This won't stop for the rest of my life.

After this devasting blow, I slowly got back into the routine of my life. I worked away all week and came home at the weekends. Now and then, I would hook up with Tameka again. Joe and Tess were happy, and Cameron surprised us when she brought a girlfriend home one night after the club; we all thought Jodie was just a friend. Well, we did until we watched them kissing each other in the pool. Yes, I became excited. What man wouldn't?

I never saw either Madison or Ethan again. I drove in the street a few months later and parked up the road. I saw Madison's car in the driveway and the Chevy blazer outside. At least Ethan is happy, I thought and drove off. This mattered more to me than the anger in my stomach towards his mother. I never went there again; it would have hurt too much. I had the urge to kill again before long and have always been able to control it. Well, up to now anyway. Tess became pregnant in November; Joe was over the moon. I was made up to see how happy Joe and Tess had become. I slept with Jess just once and acted like it was a mistake saying we were both drunk. This wasn't true; I was sober. I just wanted to see how she was between the sheets. The gang of us carried on with our lives, and this now brings me to the end of my California life.

Printed in Great Britain
by Amazon

66306874R00098